OVERLAND TRAIL

Overland Trail

by
Jenny Felix

Dales Large Print Books
Long Preston, North Yorkshire,
England.

British Library Cataloguing in Publication Data.

Felix, Jenny
  Overland trail.

  A catalogue record for this book is
  available from the British Library

  ISBN 1-85389-565-2 pbk

First published in Great Britain by The Hamlyn Publishing
Group, 1983

Copyright © 1983 by Jenny Felix

Published in Large Print July 1995 by arrangement with
Judy Turner.

Dales Large Print is an imprint of
Library Magna Books Ltd.
Printed and bound in Great Britain by
T.J. Press (Padstow) Ltd., Cornwall, PL28 8RW.

CHAPTER 1

It was a fine day, the sky a burning blue, the trees seeming to shimmer as they overhung the slow-flowing river. Charlotte Gibson stood at the rail of the *Missouri Queen*, peering ahead to where she could just see what looked like a landing stage. She narrowed her eyes beneath the brim of her bonnet. Was it St Joseph's at last? It was obviously a township of some sort, since the boat was edging nearer the bank, and even as she watched a blast on the ship's siren confirmed her hopes. This must be their destination!

'Well, looks like we've arrived, Miss Charlotte! Looks kinda busy, too. Reckon there's a waggon train leavin' soon.'

Charlotte turned and smiled at the fat middle-aged man leaning on the rail beside her.

'I hope you're right, Mr Statler; I daren't waste what little money I have left on hotel bills, so I'm hoping to join a train for California as soon as may be.'

Her companion nodded.

'That's good sense, Miss Charlotte. Soon's we git ashore you want to find a trail boss; he'll be the one to ask. Though I'm sure a pretty girl like you won't have to ask more than once!'

The boat moved out of the shelter of the trees which had hidden the landing stage and Charlotte picked up her valise, joined the line of passengers waiting to disembark and looked down at St Joseph's. It was a bustling, noisy little place. The landing stage, made of rough-hewn wooden planks, abutted directly on to a dirt road and was crowded with people, mostly men. Vividly painted signs decorated the fronts of ramshackle wooden shacks, indicating that they were hotels, gambling saloons, shops and offices, though there was not one building which looked capable of withstanding a storm of wind!

As she watched, one of the sailors aboard the *Missouri Queen* jumped ashore and made fast with ropes fore and aft, then the gangplank was lowered. Immediately, a crowd of people surged forward; there were cries, waves, shouts, and those on board began to edge towards the gangplank. Charlotte adjusted her parasol so that it shaded her face from the sunshine, grasped her valise and moved forward, knowing Mr and Mrs Statler were behind her, coping with their baggage with the aid of a young negro boy. She smiled at them, then faced the gangplank once more. She would see the Statlers again once they were ashore, for although they were not going to undertake the plains crossing, having no interest in California, they would be staying at the hotel for a night or two until their son arrived from his farm further inland to fetch them.

Once, Charlotte thought to herself as she shuffled nearer to the rail, I would have been most indignant at having to wait in a line just to disembark from a ship. But that was before she had left England, where her wishes had been of some consequence, to herself at any rate! Back in New York, when she had disembarked after the long Atlantic crossing, she had imagined the worst part of her journey over. The cramped hold of an immigrant ship was easily the most uncomfortable experience she had ever suffered, and her knowledge of the geography of the United States of America being vague, to say the least, she had not had the slightest conception that she would have to travel on by railroad, hired coach and river boat, just to reach the point from which the waggon trains left for the plains crossing to California. Nor, indeed, that a further two thousand miles of rugged, almost uninhabited country lay between her and the Golden State.

But now she was just devoutly grateful that someone had discovered gold in California and that the plains crossing was possible for anyone who wanted to join a waggon train, or how would she have reached Freddy? For this whole undertaking was for Freddy, her elder brother.

He had been wild, she acknowledged that; but not wicked. Their stepfather had disliked Freddy, found fault with him, used any excuse to make the rest of the family think badly of the boy. And when Mr Addison had found Freddy kissing Miss Annabel Brown, the young lady he earnestly desired as a wife for his own dull, stick-in-the-mud son, it had been all the excuse he needed. Freddy had been provided with a one-way ticket to America and promised an allowance for the rest of his life, provided he never returned to Liverpool.

Telling his sister afterwards, Freddy had treated the whole thing as a great lark, and a chance to get away from the hated Addison family and to make his fortune. Charlotte, knowing how desperately she would miss him, had nevertheless seen the sense of what he had said. There could be no happiness for him in Liverpool whilst their stepfather ran the family firm and put everyone against his stepson; better to make a clean break.

Charlotte had kissed Freddy goodbye tearfully, therefore, but not too despairingly. Her brother was handsome and clever; he would make his way in the New World and would send for her when he could afford to do so.

And then, out of the blue, Mr Addison had unfolded the fate he had in store for his stepdaughter. His brother, Geoffrey Addison, recently widowed, wanted a wife; he had discussed the matter thoroughly and, having noticed a wild streak in Charlotte, had decided that marriage would sober her, make her more amenable.

'Your sainted mother would have wished it,' he told Charlotte, in flagrant contradiction of the truth, for Geoffrey Addison was the wrong side of sixty and his stepdaughter barely eighteen. 'You will be married in a month, and will move into Geoffrey's town house. I trust you will remember the devoted way your Aunt Mathilda reared you, and apply the same principles in your upbringing of your husband's motherless brood, Charlotte.'

Charlotte, outwardly complacent, had made up her mind what to do between one breath and the next. She would follow Freddy to America! She could obtain money from her stepfather's safe, buy a ticket for New York, and be with Freddy before Mr Addison had realised whither she had fled.

Perhaps her stepfather's accusation of a wild streak had not been entirely unfounded, for without giving the matter any more thought Charlotte had stolen down to his study in the middle of the night, taken as much money as she could lay hands on, and made her way to the docks. Buying a steerage berth to the States in the good ship *Star of Ireland* had been well within her newly acquired means, and she had left her home and country almost without regrets. She had been kept close by the Addisons, closeted with a governess, never allowed to leave the house unchaperoned; it was strange to be independent but very pleasant, and though she had been horrified, at first, to realize that she must learn to dress herself, to cook her own stirabout, even to launder her own clothing, she was young and resilient enough to do what she had to and to pay someone to do what she found thoroughly distasteful.

'Come along, ma'am, step lively!'

The admonition came from the passenger directly behind her. Charlotte glanced over her shoulder. She caught a glimpse of a very tall man with a wide-brimmed hat shading pale, piercing eyes, then turned her head to the front once more, for it was rude to stare.

'I can't step lively,' she said pettishly. 'I've got this wretched valise in one hand, and my parasol, and I have to hold up my skirt so that I don't catch my foot in it. You'll just have to wait.'

She was at the head of the gangplank now, about to step on to it. A lean brown hand touched hers, then before she could do more than gasp had taken her valise. 'Allow me, ma'am.'

Charlotte twisted round, remembering that all her worldly possessions were in the

15

bag and that pickpockets abounded on the river boats. She tried to grab her property back, colour flooding her cheeks.

'Give me my bag at once, please! How dare you take it from me!'

He allowed her to take back the valise, but even as she regained possession of it she felt strong hands encircle her waist. She was lifted easily off her feet and crushed against the stranger's chest. Her elegant bonnet tipped forward over her nose, the pink Indian muslin skirt was crushed in his grip and her nostrils were assailed by the strong, masculine smell of leather, horses and another, unfamiliar, odour which in different circumstances, she might have found exciting, the smell of his skin and hair.

'Sir! Put me down! How dare you! *Put me down!*'

Her breathless fury and frantic wriggles had no effect whatsoever. He carried her down the gangplank and on to the quay and as the onlookers laughed he stood for one maddening moment, holding her in his arms, whilst she burned with humiliation.

'There, ma'am, down in a trice, and no one held up longer than necessary!'

He did not stand her down but loosened

his grip so that she slid through his hands until her feet touched the ground. She dropped her valise and rounded on him. How dared he let his hands slide over her like that—his fingers were still resting lightly on her waist! She stepped back, her temper rising still further.

'Get your hands off me! I'll report you! I'll...'

He was well over six foot tall, with those curiously light eyes, a high-bridged nose and a sensuous mouth. His skin was deeply tanned, making his teeth look even whiter as he smiled down at her.

'Report me? But it wasn't I who was obstructing the gangplank, ma'am.'

His hands were still at her waist and his expression showed only amusement, not a spark of remorse for her plight. She stepped back again and immediately he tightened his grip slightly. Perhaps it was that possessive movement, perhaps it was the mockery in his eyes, or perhaps it was just that someone in the crowd sniggered, but whatever the cause Charlotte's temper snapped. She drew back her hand and hit him, hard, across that self-confident and undeniably handsome face.

There was a moment of complete silence,

when the very birds seemed to stop singing and Charlotte felt sharply afraid. Across one lean cheek the marks of her fingers showed dull red. He was staring down at her, the amusement gone from his eyes, their expression cold. His mouth no longer looked sensuous, his lips were set, harsh.

'An Englishwoman's thanks! If you ever cross my path again, ma'am, I'll show you how an American repays them.'

He turned on his heel and was gone, pushing through the crowd, a head above most of the men present.

People moved, began to talk, and Charlotte was jostled out of the way by those anxious to board the river steamer. The Statlers, who must have witnessed the whole of that dreadful scene, moved towards her. Mrs Statler took her arm.

'He didn't mean no harm, Miss Charlotte! A cowhand, flown with whisky very like. A pity you slapped him, but it's soon forgot. Now let's go to the hotel and forget all about it. We could do with a cool drink, I dare say.'

Charlotte went meekly across the dirt road, dodging a team of mules dragging a waggon and weaving rather wildly from one sidewalk to the other, and into the hallway of the largest of the wooden hotel buildings. Whilst Mr Statler booked a room for himself and his wife, she mulled over the whole wretched episode of the stranger on the river boat. He had not been drunk. He had just decided to make a fool of her, picking her up like a sack of potatoes! No Englishman would treat a gently born girl in such a way! She should not have slapped his face, of course, no matter what provocation had been offered, but it had been done and now her best course was to get out of St Joseph's with all possible speed on the earliest waggon train leaving for California. It would never do to linger in the town and be accosted by the wretched man again! She shuddered at the thought.

When her turn came to speak to the clerk behind the desk, therefore, she asked him to reserve a room for her for one night, and to tell her where the waggon trains assembled. He was happy to oblige, adding that a train was to set forth next day under the aegis of an ex-officer of the American army, a man known as Wolf.

'The rest of the party's men, mind,' he cautioned her. 'It's men that want to git to the goldfields more'n women. But I daresay you won't object to that?'

There was something in his tone which made Charlotte give him a hard look but he returned her gaze frankly enough, so she picked up her valise and handed it to him for safekeeping, said goodbye to the Statlers and headed for the assembly point.

She found it easily enough by the simple expedient of following the main dirt road out of the town. Wooden buildings gave place to canvas ones, then to tents and shelters, and then, in a wide meadow beside the river, Charlotte found the waggons, with all the bustle of an impending departure surrounding them. Mules grazed on the end of ropes or roughly hobbled, carts discharged loads, men strolled around in the sunshine. No one took the slightest notice of her and Charlotte could not help but be affronted, for her white skin and coppery hair had always brought her a good deal of admiring attention from young men. However, she walked slowly amongst the waggons, searching for an office, or for someone with an air of authority.

Presently, she found someone who was at least staying in one spot, and who made no attempt to move away as she approached him. He was a short, thickset man with very black greasy hair hanging over a broad forehead, and he was checking what appeared to be supplies and heaving the sacks into a waggon standing nearby. In front of him burned a fire, and a kettle, standing beside it, seemed to indicate that he was about to make himself a drink. Charlotte, who was extremely thirsty, moved nearer to him. He was scowling at a long list which he held in one hand, and muttering to himself.

'Excuse me! Can you tell me where I might find Mr Wolf?'

The thickset man glared at her for a moment, scowled at his list again, then bent and untied the string around the neck of one of the sacks. He peered inside, then let out a stream of oaths and turned to shout at a young man in a checked shirt and corduroy trousers who was passing.

'Hey, Leo, you coma here! What this mean, stilla no macaroni? I tell you...' He lapsed into a foreign language which Charlotte recognised as Italian, his gestures becoming wilder as his obvious fury grew. The young man blinked, attempted to reason with him, and then gave a groan of dismay as the other, with a contemptuous gesture, threw the list into the fire, grabbed a dilapidated carpet bag, and set off, still shouting imprecations, in the direction of St Joseph's.

The young man who had been addressed as Leo scratched his head, then raised his shoulders in an enormous, defeated shrug. He turned to Charlotte, his expression apologetic, and grinned at her.

'Gee ma'am, wish I knew what we've done wrong this time! Giuseppe's sure a good cook, but his temper! I wonder where he's gone?'

'Back to Independence, where he's got friends who appreciate him, I believe,' Charlotte said carefully. 'I didn't mean to eavesdrop, but he was shouting so. I gather you doubted his honesty over a consignment of dried beef and then promised him macaroni which has not been forthcoming.'

Light dawned on the young man's face.

'You speak that durned lingo? When he comes back, perhaps you could tell me words to explain that I know he didn't have nothin' to do with the dried beef, it's in another waggon. As for the macaroni...'

'He isn't coming back,' Charlotte said

22

gently. 'I told you, he's gone to Independence. It's a place, I gather from what he said.'

'Aw, now Wolf'll blame me and expect me to cook the meals instead of Giuseppe,' the young man groaned. 'Well, if he does, he'll live to regret it. Here he comes!'

'Where? I've been wanting to speak to...' Charlotte swung round, following her companion's stricken glance. 'Oh no! It can't be!'

It was the man from the river boat, striding towards them, his face like a thundercloud, his hat pulled over his brow. With plenty of time to take in his appearance as he stormed towards them, Charlotte saw that he wore a doeskin jacket, breeches and highly polished riding boots. He had a whip in one hand, which he held in a businesslike manner. He called out to her companion whilst he was still some distance away.

'All right, Leo, you've done it this time! What did you say to Giuseppe? Do I have to...' He broke off as he came near enough to recognise Charlotte. Immediately his expression became saturnine. 'I'm sorry, I didn't realise you had a visitor. An Englishwoman, too!'

'I've been waiting to see you, Mr Wolf,' Charlotte said before Leo could open his mouth. 'I'm hoping to cross the plains with you, in your waggon train. I have money for the journey.'

Wolf's eyebrows rose but before he could speak Leo broke in.

'She didn't say nothin' to me about that, Wolf, or I'd have told her it waren't no use. We ain't taking no creature comforts with us.'

Charlotte's mouth fell open. Creature comforts? Whatever did he mean? But Wolf seemed to have no doubts at all. She saw his mouth curve into a hard grin.

'Very true, Leo.' He turned to Charlotte. 'Be off! Ply your trade elsewhere!'

Charlotte felt her cheeks flame. Leo must have thought she wanted to work her passage across the plains by pleasuring the men in the waggon train, as she had seen some of the sluts doing aboard the *Star of Ireland,* and Wolf was saying that he thought the same. She was glad she had slapped his face, glad she had humiliated him down on the waterfront! She gripped the handle of her parasol, her knuckles whitening. How she would like to bring it cracking down on his hateful, arrogant face!

'I'm not...' she began, then stopped. She had seen the look in those light, watchful eyes. He knew very well she was not a loose woman. He had merely made that obnoxious remark to pay her back for slapping his face. She took a deep breath. 'Mr Wolf, I was very wrong to slap your face, and you were wrong to slap my reputation, for I am not—not what you imply. But could we not consider ourselves even, now?'

'If you wish,' he said indifferently. He moved past her and began to gather up papers from the grass, throwing some of them contemptuously on to the fire, though others he kept in his hand. 'Leo, since you seem to have lost us Giuseppe, start putting the supplies into the chuck waggon. You're appointed cook.'

Leo, with a wry glance at Charlotte, began to heave the sacks on to the tail of the waggon, but although Charlotte knew she had been both snubbed and dismissed in that short sentence she lingered, hoping that the man might be persuaded to add her to his party if she promised him as much money as she and Freddy could muster when they reached California.

'Mr Wolf, if you could just listen, I have enough money for the crossing, and when we reach California, I could...'

He ignored her, continuing to gather up the papers scattered with so prodigal a hand by Giuseppe, then walked past her, evidently intending to enter the waggon. Charlotte went towards him, holding out an imploring hand.

'Sir, I need to get to California so urgently! I would be so...'

He looked up, his expression impatient and then, with a muffled exclamation, he leapt on her like a tiger, knocking her on to the grass. One moment she was standing there, prettily posed, her parasol held up to shade her from the sun, the next she was being rolled over in the grass whilst hard hands beat at her nether regions. She screamed even as he moved away from her and she received what felt like the entire Missouri river full upon her. The cold water took her breath away, cutting her scream short, and before she could give vent to any more shrieks she was being helped to her feet, wet, bedraggled, and shaking. It was then that she smelled burning.

'Better wet than a cinder, ma'am!'

She realised that she stood in the circle of the trail boss's arm and pulled away, but he pointed downwards.

'Look at yourself.'

She looked, and hastily snatched up her parasol, holding it protectively over the gaping hole that had been burnt in her skirt and petticoats. As she stepped towards Wolf to plead with him, she realized, the fire must have licked up her skirt, devouring a panel before she had noticed anything was amiss.

'Oh!' she said faintly. 'I felt nothing! Indeed, I had no idea I was on fire until...'

Wolf grinned.

'Until I fell on you? It must have been quite a shock, but better than finding oneself a living torch. Can you cook? Launder clothing? Ride a mule?'

The abrupt change of subject brought her mouth open in a gape. To cover her surprise she said stiffly: 'Thank you for quenching the flames, sir. Why do you ask if I can cook?'

Before answering he dismissed Leo, with an injunction to give Matt a hand with the mules, then turned to Charlotte and took hold of her wrist. She felt she could scarcely object since he had just saved her life, and in any case his grasp was coolly impersonal, so she followed him to the entrance of the waggon into which Leo had been tumbling the sacks of food.

'See that? Our supplies for the journey. Giuseppe was to cook and wash for us, and see that the food lasted, but now he's gone. If you can take his place and do his work then you can come with us. I won't charge you for your place in the train.'

Charlotte had never boiled a kettle or rinsed a stocking in her life until she took passage for New York. Even then she had done little but heat soup and pay someone else to launder her clothing. But this did not deter her. Anyone could cook, and she certainly did not intend to lose such an opportunity for a mere scruple!

'I'll do it. I'll cook for you, and do the washing.'

'Good.' He nodded, obviously assuming that she could do as she claimed. 'I'll come into St Joe's with you and buy the essentials you'll need. You've enough money?' And at her eager nod. 'Good. You've got some sensible clothing?'

She glanced ruefully at her ruined skirt.

French Muslin was not, perhaps, sensible, but it was expensive!

'I'll get some.'

'And you must be back here by five o'clock tomorrow morning.'

'Five! But how shall I wake? Will someone at the hotel wake me?'

He grinned as though at a private joke. He looked rather nice when he grinned, she reflected.

'You'll wake!'

She knew what he meant at four-thirty next morning. It was barely light, the sky scarcely paler than the land, but the racket in the hotel could be heard, she thought, streets away. Plainly, a good many guests beside herself were leaving with the waggon train!

She got out of bed and dressed in the new gown she had bought to replace the French muslin. It was a dark blue batiste, the flounces trimmed with blond lace, and had been a little more expensive than she had anticipated, but she comforted herself with the recollection that she was to work her passage, so could afford it.

Now, she tightened the narrow ribbon

around the waist and looked with satisfaction at the result of wearing her best stays. A seventeen-inch span had been achieved, even if she did feel breathless when she exerted herself, and the skirt, spread over her padded, whaleboned petticoat, was so fashionably wide that she had to sidle through the door.

She ate a hasty breakfast in the hotel dining-room amongst a crowd of men who ate quickly and ignored her, then made her way through the quiet, grey-tinted streets towards the waggon train. As she walked past the now silent shops, she remembered yesterday's shopping expedition. Wolf had made her buy a bedroll, a waterproof cape and a light rifle, as well as two pairs of boots so stout and serviceable that she hated them already. The injunction, as he left her, to spend what was left of her money on 'sensible clothes' she ignored. She had no idea what he meant anyway, so, having purchased the blue batiste gown which happened to exactly match her eyes, she had a meal of bread and cheese and fruit, and then went straight to bed. All seemed to be going according to plan.

How far this was from the truth appeared as she threaded her way amongst the waggons. Wolf was busy, shouting, commanding, helping the men to back the mules into the shafts. When he saw her he hurried over, looking far from pleased.

'What nonsense is this? How can you ride a mule in that skirt?'

She blinked at him, realizing with a stab of dismay that he had mentioned riding a mule and that she had not got a riding habit with her.

'Oh! Well, I should have removed my petticoats but I'll do so tomorrow, and then I'm sure I'll manage. You have a lady's saddle, of course?'

He stared at her, his expression forbidding.

'Did you not buy yourself one? Of course we've not got such a thing. You'll just have to learn to ride astride, and you'll have to do something about those clothes. You can't ride or walk across the plains with twenty pounds of clothing on your back! Here, you'd best sit on the waggon's tail until we stop for food, and then we'll see.'

As he finished speaking his hands went round her waist, lifting her on to the end of the waggon, and than he slung her valise in beside her.

'Stay there until I fetch you down.'

Soon enough the whole waggon train was on the move. There was a creaking, a good deal of shouting, a dog barked, and they set off into the pale mist of early morning. Sitting on the waggon's tail with her legs swinging over the side and the brand-new early morning smell of the country in her nostrils, Charlotte felt deep contentment. She was on the last stage of her journey and she had read that the plains could be crossed in sixty days. Soon she would be seeing Freddy, and they would start their new life together!

CHAPTER 2

Charlotte spent the first few hours of the journey remembering, though not regretting, her life in her stepfather's house. She had been pampered to an extent, of course, for it had been her dead mama's money which had provided the house and her long gone grandpa's fortune which had started the shipping business which Mr Addison had taken over so completely, but it had not been the pampering given to a much-loved daughter but rather the grudging duty of a reluctant stepfather.

The young Addisons and the two little Gibsons had never got on, for the children of Mr Addison's first marriage were like their father, dull, self-righteous and penny-pinching, whereas the young Gibsons took after their easy-going, fun-loving mother. What had possessed her to marry Mr Addison was more than Charlotte could begin to understand, but she did know that her mother had regretted it, long before her death seven years earlier.

'He'll devote himself to the business, and that means you and Freddy will gain by it in the long run,' her mother had assured Charlotte. 'He wouldn't push his own children ahead of mine, I'm sure of it.'

But that, of course, was precisely what he had done. And then to suggest that she must marry his horrid old brother, with his bulbous nose veined by a thousand bottles of port, and his draggly white moustache yellowed by a thousand pinches of snuff! Her mother had detested her brother-in-law and had scarcely tried to veil her feelings. A man with a dozen whining, ill-bred children and a downtrodden little wife who got more kicks than kisses, Geoffrey had not been welcome in her beautiful house in Sir Thomas Street, or in the lovely manor house in Crosby which had been her first husband's favourite home.

'No, Mr Addison, your brother must learn to treat his wife with more respect before he visits us here,' she had remarked several times, in Charlotte's hearing. 'I won't have a man like that under my roof.'

Gradually, before her death, she had begun to notice Mr Addison's insidious pushing forward of his own sons, and his constant complaints against Freddy. But by then she was a sick woman and there was little she could do, save to bring her older sister, Mathilda, to the house and try to impress on her the necessity to 'take care of my children, when I'm gone'.

But Mathilda was a spinster who wanted very much to be a married woman. She agreed with everything Mr Addison said, saw that cook made all his favourite dishes, waited on him herself. To be sure, she sometimes complained timidly over the more flagrant injustices, but she soon realized that such behaviour would do her cause no good.

Alone, the two Gibson children had struggled to grow up as their mother would have wished. And now we will do it, because we shan't have the Addisons ruining everything all the time, Charlotte told herself, sitting on the waggon's tail in the strengthening sunshine. Freddy and I will be so happy together!

'Down with you now, Miss Charlotte!'

The words broke into her reverie and she jumped, then looked down into Wolf's tanned face.

'What? Why should I get down now? Are we stopping?'

'I told you you'd ride a mule once we got going. Now's the time.'

'Ride?' Charlotte stared at him incredulously, her voice rising to a squeak. 'Without a sidesaddle? You must be mad!'

'Don't sit there arguing with me. Get down when you're told.'

The command in his voice did not endear him any further to Charlotte, who tightened her lips but remained where she was.

'Down I said, ma'am, and down I

meant. Every waggon's carefully balanced with the maximum load the team can take. You're tilting this one down at the back. Come on!'

He was grasping the bridle of a mule and now she saw that, nearby, Leo hovered, holding the reins of the tall stallion she had seen Wolf mounting as they set off. She glared down at him, wondering if he would resort to physical violence if she refused to move, and decided that he would. Sulkily she slithered down on to the ground, rucking her skirt up round her calves, hating him for making her look a fool for the second time in two days.

'Now! Gather up your skirt, and...' He gave an exclamation of annoyance. 'Take off those petticoats!'

'No, I can't!' Charlotte's hand flew to her mouth. 'The mule has no sidesaddle in any case!'

Leo, she noticed, had made himself scarce and the two of them were now well in the rear of the party, with nobody to see, nobody to rescue her. She glanced round wildly. They were in undulating meadlowland and trees in fresh leaf hid a river or stream; she could hear it chattering over its rocky bed. Before she had thought the countryside beautiful. Now it just seemed empty. Wolf stood in front of her, one hand gripping the mule's bridle close to its mouth. The other suddenly shot out and seized her by the wrist.

'Who shall take them off? You or I? You're going to ride this mule!'

She gazed up at him. He meant it. There was determination in every line of his face. She tried one more gambit.

'I—I'll lead the mule, that'll help me to walk more quickly. Just until a sidesaddle can be procured. Will that do?'

He thrust the mule's bridle into her hand and she thought, with sick relief that he had taken her point.

'Hold that and don't let go.'

She took the bridle and with both hands occupied, felt her skirt wrenched up. She shrieked, letting go the bridle as his hands almost met round her waist beneath the flounced skirt. The mule, startled by the shriek, kicked up its heels and trotted after the waggons even as Wolf ripped the boned petticoat from waistband to hem.

'There! No more nonsense, or I'll strip the rest off.'

She had scarcely started to tell him what she thought of him when he caught her wrist and began to chase the mule, dragging her behind him, tripping and stumbling over the uneven ground.

'Shut your mouth and run. I want you aboard that mule,' was the only answer he gave to her breathless, bitter protestations about his behaviour.

Leo, watching from afar, spurred after the mule, grabbed at the bridle and brought the animal back to them, and then, after an uneasy glance at Wolf and another at Charlotte, rode ahead once more. It was plain he wanted no part in the vigorous argument that he saw was to come!

But Wolf did not intend to argue. Ignoring her stuttered refusal to mount, he calmly lifted her into the high-fronted saddle. With a mere five petticoats beneath her skirt and not one of them padded or boned, it was still impossible to sit the mule with anything like dignity. A seam ripped. Charlotte kicked out wildly at Wolf's chest and received a stinging slap across her bare arm. She tried to heave her skirt down and then cried out as Wolf grabbed her boot and attempted to force it into the stirrup. At last, with tears of rage streaming down her cheeks, she managed to get her leg over the mule's back and slid on to the ground on the opposite side of the animal from Wolf. Reading retribution in his narrowed eyes, she banged her fist on the mule's saddle and yelled at him with all her strength.

'Leave me alone! I cannot ride this creature in my skirts! Don't you see, you stupid man, it isn't *won't,* it's *cannot!*'

She knew her cheeks were scarlet from their struggle, her hair was down in a glistening coppery flood, her eyes drowned blue pools as tears welled over. Even in her distress it crossed her mind that few men could have resisted her at such a moment.

It appeared, however, that Wolf's resistance was stronger than most. He swore, not gently, then walked round to her side of the mule.

'I see that. Well, you'll have to find something in your valise which will enable you to ride astride in comfort. Understand?'

She lifted her chin.

'I've nothing suitable, no riding habit, nothing. Do you expect me to own a pair of breeches?'

His eyes flickered insultingly over her figure, then he grinned.

'You wear drawers. I remember seeing them when I tore your petticoat off. Better than nothing, I daresay!'

She stormed away, dragging the mule, hating him. How could he continually mock her in this fashion! Nothing would persuade her to ride a mule astride in either her panataloons or breeches! She would just have to walk!

When a halt was called because the sun was low in the sky, Charlotte was bitterly regretting her inability to ride the mule. It was a pretty, biddable animal and though clinging on to the saddle, with the bridle looped over her arm, helped her to keep up a good pace, she was exhausted and far in the rear of the waggons when a halt was called.

Wolf rode out to meet her, a frown on his face.

'What the use of a cook who hasn't even kindled a fire? Get into camp at the double!'

She ignored him, too tired to even pretend to hurry, but he wasted no time trying to persuade her. He leaned over and gave the mule a cut across the rump with his whip. With the best will in the world,

Charlotte could not have kept up with her mount as the poor beast leapt forward and raced towards the camp.

Charlotte picked herself up from the ground. Her knees were bruised and now she would have to walk unaided into camp. She turned to give Wolf a piece of her mind and found him riding down upon her. She yelped and dodged, but he bent down and swept her up before him across the saddle, for all the world, she thought resentfully, as Young Lochinvar was said to have seized his bride.

'You're tired out. Tomorrow you must ride the mule!'

His mouth was close to her head, she could feel the breath warmly stirring the smooth crown of her hair as he spoke. She tightened her lips, however, and did not reply. They reached the camp and he slid her down on to the grass.

'Leo's laying the fire for you. Go and help him.'

She made her way towards the fire, which Leo had coaxed into a bright flame. He glanced up at her, then looked quickly away.

'Guess you'll be too tired tonight to do much, Miss Charlotte, so I'm cookin' up

41

dried peas and beef in a stew, and we'll use the bread we got in St Joe's. You kin make coffee whilst they eat.'

Charlotte squatted down and looked into the steaming pot. She made the only culinary remark she knew how to make.

'Did you put some salt in?'

'Jeez, no! How much does it need?'

She blinked, then pushed back a strand of hair with a shaking hand. How much, for goodness sake? She would have to guess.

'A pinch!' she suggested without much hope, and watched him put a tiny pinch of salt into the pot. 'A pinch for each person, I meant,' she amended hastily.

Leo seemed to take this as gospel and began throwing pinches of salt into the pot, counting as he did so. He reached twenty-five, to Charlotte's horror, before stopping.

'Twenty-five people? Oh, Leo, how can I possibly cook for so many?'

Leo glanced uneasily around him in the golden light of the setting sun.

'Don't say that, Miss Charlotte, Wolf thinks you kin manage easy! You must've seen there were a good few of us when...' He broke off. 'Here he comes!'

Charlotte's heart lurched. She grabbed a knife and began to slice one of the long loaves into uneven pieces. Wolf strode up and stood for a moment, looking down at her.

'Busy?'

She ignored him for a second and in that second, he moved. Quickly, aware of the implied threat in his attitude as he stood over her, she spoke.

'Yes. We're making a stew.'

'Leave the rest to Leo and come with me.'

Fear knifed through her. What did he want with her this time? Not another dreadful riding lesson on the mule?

'I can't. I'm busy...'

He took her by the elbows and pulled her to her feet, his hands gripping cruelly tight.

'When I say come with me, it's an order. I'm in charge here and you obey my orders, as the men do. Leo can manage without you for a bit.' He marched her over to the waggon, then leaned in and grabbed her valise. 'Come along, there's a river beyond those trees. You're going to get out of those filthy, torn clothes and into something fresh when you've had a good wash. Got another gown in here?'

He indicated the valise and she nodded, relieved that she was going to be given the opportunity to put on fresh clothing.

'That would be nice. If you'll show me where I may bathe I'll go by myself.'

He checked in his stride and raised his brows quizzically.

'By yourself? What about Indians? Prowlers from the camp? Wild animals? Or aren't you afraid of such things?'

It would have been cowardly to have said 'I'm even more afraid of you', though at that moment it would have been no more than the truth. Instead, she nodded.

'Of course, I'd not thought. Lead on, then.'

They went through the trees which had hidden the river from them and emerged where the fast running water widened into a deep pool. The bank was steep here, so that a bather could step straight into three or four feet of water, and there were bushes growing quite near the edge which Wolf indicated with a jerk of the head.

'Into the bushes and strip; don't worry, I won't look. Then straight into the water, wash and out. I'll leave your valise between the bank and the bushes, so you can climb

44

out and dress without my seeing you.' He looked down at her, the light eyes half-veiled by heavy lids. 'I've warned the men off, but they can be unscrupulous; you'll be safer with me to keep a look-out.'

He put the valise down in the shelter of the bushes and handed her a bar of soap, then hung a large linen towel over the branches nearest the water. He nodded towards the trees.

'I'll stand over there, with my back to you, until you call.'

She murmured agreement but eyed his broad shoulders uncertainly as he strode away. Would he really keep his word or would he spy on her? Though to do him justice he had shown no prurient interest when he was ripping off her one and only crinolined petticoat! His interest in her, in fact, seemed solely that of an officer with an unsatisfactory subordinate in his command! Comforted by this thought, she began to undress.

She stripped to drawers and chemisette, then went to the bank. Dabbling one toe in the water, she glanced back. She could see him clearly, his light clothing showing up well against the dark trees. He had his back to her and seemed intent on

45

something before him. At any rate, he was keeping his word.

She sat down on the bank and lowered her legs into the tepid water. It beckoned irresistibly. A quick glance over her shoulder showed he was still unmoving. Quickly, before she could change her mind, she pulled off her chemisette and then wriggled out of her drawers. Naked as a newborn babe, she slid into the water.

It was every bit as lovely as she had anticipated, cooling but not cold, caressing her heated skin. She waded out midstream, then glanced back. He still had his back to her. She ducked under, then came up and began to soap herself, turning the water opalescent as she rinsed off the suds.

When she was clean once more she turned towards the bank. Then she froze. He was kneeling on the edge of the water, looking across at her! She ducked noisily within a split second of seeing him, her hands flying protectively to her breasts, but he took no notice whatsoever. She might have been invisible. He gathered something up in his hands—she could not see what—then stood up and swung on his heel, returning to his former position facing the trees.

It was then that she remembered her drawers and chemisette, in a crumpled heap on the bank. Had he merely come down to the bank to move them back with the rest of her belongings? Heartened, she scrambled out of the water. Reaching up for the towel, she wrapped it decorously round herself, picked up the valise and clicked it open—then caught her breath. It was empty save for a thin cotton shirt and a pair of breeches. For a moment she was completely confused. Had she picked up the wrong valise, got hold of someone else's belongings by mistake?

Then, in a blinding flash, she saw it all. He had put the clothes into her valise before even coming to fetch her to bathe! That was why he had been forced to come down to the bank, so that she could not outwit him by refusing to put the clean things on and dressing in her worn and dirty gown instead. She had been chilly when she first left the water but now anger warmed her. How dared he dictate her choice of clothing in such a high-handed manner! And where were her own clothes, the lovely green silk gown which she was saving for her reunion with her brother, the brand new blue batiste gown, with only a seam torn and the skirt draggled? Where were the stays, petticoats, and chemisettes? She could not wear breeches and a shirt, showing off her shape like a wicked circus girl, and nor would she!

Standing there, towel-draped, she glanced towards him. He was still there, his broad-shouldered figure easily seen against the trees.

'Wolf!'

He turned at once and came loping towards her like his namesake. She could read amusement in his face, though his mouth was unsmiling.

'Yes, ma'am? You ready to go back?'

He stopped within three feet of her, his dark brows shooting up in well-simulated surprise.

'What's this? Still not dressed?'

'Where, sir, are my clothes?'

He passed a hand across his mouth, then indicated the valise.

'In there.'

'No. They belong to someone else.'

'They're yours. I paid over the money for them myself.'

'How kind!' Her tone fairly throbbed with sarcasm. 'And now, if you please, would you give me my gown and petticoats, and my—my underthings.'

'No.'

The small, cold word dropped like a stone into the silence, leaving her hopes shattered. What could she do against such a flat denial? But she did not intend to let the matter rest there!

'Why not?'

'Because I've burnt them.'

'You *burnt* them? You dared to burn my beautiful clothes? My petticoats and ribbons, and my satin sandals? You burnt them all?'

'That's right. And your—your under-things as well.'

There was a ghost of a smile on his mouth now as well as in his eyes and it was that which brought her flying across the short space which separated them, hatred and helplessness combining to make her reckless.

'You beast! I hate you!'

She slapped his dark, mocking face with all her force, and found herself pulled tight against him, helplessly imprisoned in his arms.

'That was foolish, wasn't it!' She was suddenly aware of her near nakedness, the flimsiness of the towel between them.

She struggled to free herself but he held her without effort. 'You owe me a debt already. This is the second time you've slapped my face.'

She stood quite still, knowing the uselessness of struggling, aware that her behaviour had been more than foolish, it had been downright provocative. She looked up into his face and put on her most pleading expression.

'Please give me my clothes, Wolf!'

He shook his head, enjoying her discomfiture.

'They've gone, ma'am. And now I'll take what's owing.'

He bent his head and his lips found hers. She pushed against his chest, and his hands traversed her back, smoothing the satin skin, reminding her yet again that the towel around her was scarcely any impediment, should he... She stopped trying to pull back and he moved his mouth, suddenly more demanding, forcing her lips apart for his invasion, deepening the kiss, and suddenly her resistance fled and she felt an answering surge of passion so that, for a moment, she clung to him, a willing victim as he plundered her mouth without mercy.

50

When he put her away from him she felt clinging and softened, wanting tenderness from him, forgetting that the kiss had been a punishment rather than a shared experience. His arms still encircled her and in the dusk she could see the sardonic expression on his face. Immediately, she remembered that he had kissed her to hurt and annoy and not to enchant her. She hated herself for that brief moment when she had clung, had enjoyed his caresses. She glared up at him, trying to infuse into her voice all her annoyance, hoping that he had not noticed the softening effect of his kiss.

'You had no right to destroy my dresses, and I won't wear men's clothes!'

'Then go naked. I'm going back to the camp.'

It was dusk now, the sky blooming deep blue, the first stars pricking the approaching night. The woods looked menacing. Charlotte clutched his arm.

'Wait! All right, I'll wear these clothes, but only till I can get myself a proper riding habit.'

He ignored the half-hearted threat but turned his back on her and stood, hat tipped on the back of his head, legs apart, hands low on hips, gazing towards the distant flames of the campfire which could be seen between the trees and whistling a tune beneath his breath. She reached for the breeches and he said: 'Get a move on, now.'

She found that she feared being left more than she feared looking foolish in the breeches. She hurried, desperately dragging on the clothes, then said, still buttoning the shirt, 'Ready.'

He turned, eyeing her appraisingly.

'Good. No one will mistake you for a young man but you look sensibly clad for crossing the plains on a mule.'

'I suppose you're right.' She sighed and picked up her empty valise. 'Shall we go back now?'

Without another word he took her elbow in his hand to guide her through the trees and Charlotte, at his touch, felt again for one moment that tightening of the stomach muscles combined with another, more complex feeling which had assailed her when he had kissed her so savagely. She tensed, then chided herself. Once they had eaten she would be able to sleep and forget the trials and tribulations of the day. And also the painful pleasure which she had known in his arms.

When they reached the encampment the tents were set up and Leo was handing round plates of stew and hunks of bread. She took her portion eagerly, for her bathe had made her hungry, and squatted down beside Leo.

'Where do I sleep, Leo? Did Giuseppe have a tent which I might use?'

The fair-haired young man looked embarrassed and turned his head away, muttering. Charlotte sighed. What was the matter now?

'Do tell me where I'm to sleep! I didn't buy a tent. I thought...'

Wolf interrupted her, bringing his plate of stew over and sitting down beside her. 'You'll sleep in the waggon. That one.' He pointed with his knife. 'Your bedroll's already in there.'

She saw Leo's eyes widen and something in his glance made her colour up to the roots of her hair. She saw his mouth begin to open, saw Wolf shoot a glance across that silenced him. Charlotte turned to her food and began to eat. It was no use worrying or trying to interpret what the little exchange had meant. Men were strange creatures. And at least she now knew where she was to sleep.

Wolf left them whilst she was pouring coffee into tin mugs and Leo explained that he was arranging watches, for though the grass here was rich and good and the beasts could be tethered yet still get plenty of grazing, it was necessary for a watch to be kept so that neither marauding animals nor Indians—nor their fellow-travellers—might interfere with their beasts or attempt to steal from the waggons.

'At least the cheeses will be safe,' Charlotte remarked crossly when Wolf rejoined them and bade her make her way to her waggon. 'For I see I'm sharing my accommodation with a dozen or so of the things. I shall reek of cheese in the morning.'

'It'll blow away once you get aboard that mule,' Wolf said unsympathetically, but Leo lingered, his freckled face friendly in the fireglow. 'Them breeches suit you fine, Miss Charlotte, and don't you worry that it's demeaning, 'cos many a female takes to male clothes to cross the plains.'

'Truly? Thanks for telling me, Leo. It does make me feel less self-conscious.' She shot a malevolent glance at Wolf, then turned towards her waggon. 'Well, I'm off to bed, and no doubt I'll sleep sound, even if it's only because I've been rendered unconscious by the smell of cheese!'

The last thing she heard as she climbed into the waggon was Wolf's soft laugh.

CHAPTER 3

'Wake up, Miss Charlotte!'

Leo's voice brought Charlotte's eyes blinking open. She listened, but heard nothing further, and her lids drooped over her eyes once more; she must have imagined the voice.

'Miss Charlotte!'

Sighing, she crawled to the end of the waggon and stuck her head out of the gap in the lacing. Dawn was cool and grey outside, the grass furred with a heavy dew. Leo stood there, his freckled face anxious.

'Oh, Miss Charlotte, Wolf said to wake you. He wants you to start breakfast, then I'm to finish it whilst he gives you a lesson in riding astride.'

'Oh. All right, I shan't be a minute.'

Charlotte withdrew, thoughtfully, into the waggon and began to dress. She had no desire to cook breakfast, nor the faintest idea how to set about such a thing, but neither did she want to be given a riding lesson by the trail boss! To have to do both seemed very unfair. Was there not some way to get out of one or other task?

She brushed her hair until it bushed out round her head in a coppery halo, then tied it back and stepped down from the waggon. No one else was stirring. Wolf was crouched by the fire, pushing what looked like lumps of dough into the heart of it, and Leo was pouring steaming water into three mugs. It was surprisingly chilly and she shivered, clasping her arms about herself.

'I'd best go back to the waggon and put a blanket round my shoulders; I'm cold.'

Wolf stood up, stretched, then shook his head.

'You can't ride in a blanket. I'll lend you a jacket.'

His tent had already been struck but his saddle-bags stood nearby and he reached into one of them, then brought over to her a jacket similar to the one he was wearing. Soft, supple doeskin slipped warmly round her shoulders and from it rose the odour that she associated with Wolf and no one else. It was like having his arms round her, and she tried very hard to hate the idea.

'Show Leo how to make porridge, Charlotte, then we'll go.'

That was enough to reanimate plenty of resentment! She shot him a venomous glance. Why should she pretend, when she would only be found out?

'I can't make porridge. Or stew. Or coffee. I can't make anything. Young ladies in England aren't taught such things. When I said I'd cook for you I meant I'd—I'd sort of supervise. Warm soup over the fire. Not actually cook.'

'You conceited, useless little bitch!' Contempt shone from his eyes. 'Take that look off your face or I'll make you regret it!'

Her sneer had been partly bravado but the threat spoken so coldly and quietly frightened her into dropping even the pretence of defiance. She bent down and dragged the big pot nearer to the fire.

'I'm sorry. I'll try! I didn't mean...'

He crossed over to stand beside her, then picked up the bucket of water which stood nearby and poured some of it into the pot.

57

'Watch carefully, because this is your first and last lesson in cooking porridge. And presently, I'll show you how to make dampers.'

He told her that 'dampers' were lumps of dough, baked in the heart of the fire, then brought out when they were risen and eaten with butter and syrup. He proved to be a patient teacher, though as he had threatened he only told her how to do a thing once, and then expected her to get it right. When the first dampers had been brought out of the fire and eaten, he stood up. His voice cracked like a whip lash.

'Get the mule!'

She ran to the lines where the mules were tethered, untied her mule, Tandy, and hurried back to Wolf who waited for her, the saddle and bridle on his arm.

'Keep hold of her halter and watch.'

He saddled and bridled the animal, then removed the gear and handed it to her.

'Now you do it.'

She fumbled at first, doing up straps wrong, trying to fasten the belly band without putting her knee in the mule's belly first, to force it to release the air which swelled its sides. He showed her how, if she did not make the animal release the air, the saddle would just slip round underneath it the first time any strain was put on it, which made sense to Charlotte.

She got it right at last and he lifted her into the saddle with such gusto that she very nearly landed on the far side of the animal. Lurching upright again, she cast him a fulminating glance which he did not even notice, since he was mounting his stallion. As soon as he was in the saddle he wheeled his mount and joined her, grabbing her reins and pulling her mule into a trot.

'Grip with your knees! Now rise to the trot. No, not right up in the air, I don't want to see light between your breeches and the saddle. That's better. Keep your hands *down*, woman, and don't jerk at the animal's mouth like that!'

Riding astride, she decided presently, was easier than riding sidesaddle, though quite different. It was not long before she was able to snatch the reins back from Wolf, dig her heels into Tandy's sides and make off across the grassland at a gallop. His great stallion rode her down without difficulty but when he caught her up Wolf was smiling.

'You've proved your point; you can handle the mule. Now back to the camp.'

She hesitated, wondering whether to gallop on, defying him, to enjoy more of the rolling grasslands, the cool morning air, but a quick glance through her lashes brought her obediently round. It was all too obvious that Wolf was used to giving orders and having them immediately obeyed, and it would do no good to annoy him by deliberately flouting his authority. She longed for the moment when they arrived in California though, and she could tell Freddy what a dictatorial, arrogant beast the trail boss was, and see Freddy cut him down to size. But at this point doubt seized her; Freddy was tall and strong enough, but he must be a dozen years younger than the trail boss. It might not be wise to try to encourage Freddy to challenge Wolf!

She slipped off the mule and went towards the campfire, where Leo was clearing up after the men's breakfast and getting everything packed back into the waggons so that they could move on before the sun grew hot.

'We're a bit disorganized still,' Leo said as they laced the front of the waggon closed. 'When we were in Cuba...'

'In Cuba? What were you doing there? And who's we?'

Leo climbed down from the waggon and fetched the bucket of water, which he proceeded to sprinkle over the fire.

'Always do this before you move on,' he instructed her. 'You can't just let a fire die, because a fire could starve out those coming along behind.' When the fire was thoroughly doused he continued with his explanation. 'In the Spanish-American war, Wolf was the captain of my company. The war ended just as gold was discovered in California and Wolf decided to make up a party to try for a stake. Everyone in the waggon train was in the platoon.' He grinned at her ruefully. 'Except for you, ma'am!'

'Is that why no one wanted me?' They were going to be the last people to leave the site for even Wolf was mounting Stormbird and spurring off in pursuit of the rest of the waggons. 'Did you feel soldiers were best on their own?'

Leo's horse and Tandy were still tethered to the last waggon; Leo untied them, watched the driver get the clumsy vehicle moving, then mounted his horse. He frowned down at Charlotte, already on

61

her mule, still wary of talking too freely to her, she guessed.

'Wolf not said anything to you?'

'Wolf tells me nothing, except how I must ride, dress, and comport myself.'

She sounded as resentful as she felt, but took no offence when he grinned.

'That's military discipline, Miss Charlotte. You'll get used to it. No, Wolf laid down there was to be no women along. He said the men didn't have women in Cuba, and if we brought 'em they'd cause fights. See?'

'You mean c-camp followers,' Charlotte said, her cheeks beginning to burn. 'I'm just a traveller, on my way to California to live with my brother, that's all.'

'That so? Does Wolf know?'

'I don't think I mentioned Freddy, but he knows I'm not a camp follower!'

Leo's eyebrows rose and his skin reddened.

'You sure, Miss Charlotte?'

'I suppose I can't be sure,' Charlotte admitted. 'But if he thought me a bad woman, why did he let me join the waggon train? No, I'm sure he thinks me what I am—a respectable lady travelling to California.'

Leo cleared his throat.

'I guess we Americans seem pretty unconventional to you, is that so, Miss Charlotte?'

'A little, perhaps. Why?'

'Because we ain't. Not where our womenfolk's concerned. No respectable gal your age 'ud run off and join a company of men!'

Charlotte gripped the reins tightly and felt the colour burn into her cheeks again. The sun was up now, and she hoped Leo would think she was growing warm.

'I wouldn't have done so had there been any alternative,' she said defensively. 'But my money ran out and I can't earn any more, and I simply *must* join my brother. I told him in a letter that I was setting out and he'll worry dreadfully if I don't arrive soon.'

'Run away from home, did you?'

'Yes, I did. I was to marry a horrible old man—my stepfather had sent Freddy away, so there was no one to take my part—and I could not bear it, really I could not. He's over sixty and has a dozen children, and he killed his first wife! If Freddy had known he would have forbidden it, but...' Her voice trailed away.

'Killed his first wife? Gee, that's...'

Hurriedly Charlotte disillusioned him.

'Caused to die, I should have said. Leo, do *you* think I'm a—a bad sort of woman? Is that what the other men think?'

'I thought you were Wolf's woman, at first,' Leo said frankly. 'But when I saw that you slept in the waggon and Wolf in his tent...' He coloured, staring steadfastly ahead between his horse's pricked ears. 'Well, guess I knew I was mistaken. But the others probably think Wolf goes visitin', I guess.'

'Well, he doesn't, and he'd get a very unexpected reception if he did,' Charlotte said tartly. 'I wish you'd tell the others, Leo...'

But at this point Wolf called for Leo to join him and Charlotte found herself alone. She was humiliated to know that the men thought her Wolf's mistress, but she told herself they were only ignorant soldiers whose opinion mattered not at all. What mattered was to reach California, and Freddy!

That evening, it rained. And continued to rain for two days and nights, so that the camp was perpetually cold and wet. Men sat dismally round the spitting fire draped in their waterproofs to eat, then went early to bed.

But the third day was dry and they rode out at dawn since Wolf wanted them to stop at a trading post that night. He had been silent and taciturn during the spell of wet weather, but riding beside Charlotte as the sun rose he became almost talkative.

'We'll stop for coffee and a bite in an hour,' he said, shading his hand to look up at the sun, climbing the cloudless sky. 'Then I'm going to give you a shooting lesson. I hope you won't need to use the gun, but it's best that you know how.'

'I don't mind being taught to shoot,' Charlotte said. 'I'll probably be very good at it. I was very good at archery.'

A sardonic eyebrow climbed.

'Yeah? Well, we'll see how you manage a gun.'

True to his word, he allowed her to gulp down her hot coffee and snatch a mouthful of bread and corned beef when they stopped, then hauled her off for a shooting lesson. They had stopped near a stream, on the banks of which immensely tall beeches grew. With the sunshine the birds had grown bold and tuneful once

65

more and early summer was evident in the lush grass and flowers and the sweetness of the air. The beeches, in vivid leaf, cast their dappled shade on Wolf and Charlotte as they strolled away from the main camp to a clear part of the bank, where Wolf set up a pile of tins for a target before returning to her side.

'D'you know how to hold a gun?'

She shook her head. Her bright hair was tied back with a thin piece of satin ribbon, she wore her white shirt and dun-coloured breeches and knew she looked workmanlike and sensible, a far cry from the pampered young lady with her parasol and voluminous skirts who had thought herself so fine barely a week earlier.

'Then I'll show you.'

He put the gun into her hands then stood behind her, bringing the gun up slowly, placing her hands in the right positions on stock and barrel. This meant that his arms had to be round her and she was pressed against his chest, feeling the thud of his heart somewhere in the region of her left shoulder blade. His cheek was close to hers and she could feel his dark hair brushing her temple. Her pulses began to race and she sighted along the

66

barrel, trying to concentrate on the job in hand and ignore the effect his closeness had on her.

'Is this right?' Her voice was breathless and he moved away from her, his eyes going shrewdly from the angle of the barrel to the target.

'Bring the barrel down a bit. That's fine.' He moved until he was standing directly behind her, his chest grazing her back. 'Now fire!'

She fired and the gun jerked back into her shoulder, pushing her into his arms. He caught and steadied her, then showed her how to reload.

'You weren't ready for the recoil. Next time, remember it kicks back and allow for the barrel jerking up a bit. Fire low.'

She fired again and this time scattered the tins.

After forty minutes she was tired and wanted to stop, but he would not let her. 'I want you to be able to bring that barrel up, steady her, fire and reload without thinking about it. When you're tired, when you're soaked through with rain, when you've only just come awake. And that only comes with practice.'

Whilst she had been shooting she had

noticed, on the opposite side of the stream, an object perched high in the branches of a tall beech tree. It was smallish, square, definitely not animate. She waited until her gun was loaded and Wolf was standing back watching her, then spoke.

'Wolf? See the thing in that tree?'

He narrowed his eyes and followed her gaze.

'I see it.'

'Watch me hit it with my first bullet!'

She squeezed the trigger gently, as he had taught her, and even as the bullet exploded from the barrel he knocked the gun up so that the shot whistled harmlessly into the air and the recoil caught Charlotte beneath the chin like the kick of a mule. Charlotte found herself flat on her back with Wolf, far from apologising for his strange behaviour, bending over her with murder in his eyes.

'You little fool! You don't know how lucky you are!' He dragged her roughly to her feet, then began to march her towards the stream.

'It's only an old box, and I think you've broken my jaw! What on earth did you do that for?'

She sounded more aggrieved than furious,

subdued by his unexpected reaction. Also, pain was making her feel sick and stupid.

'I'll show you why I did it.'

They reached the edge of the stream and she dragged back.

'Not over there. I don't want to get my boots and breeches soaked!'

He pointed further upstream, to where a fallen tree-trunk formed a bridge over the water.

'We're crossing there.'

When they reached the tree-trunk he put her in front of him, steadying her with his hands at her waist, and they crossed safely. Once on the far bank he almost trotted her to the foot of the tree with the box-like object in its branches. She was cross now, the pain in her jaw giving her great discomfort, but curiosity was still there. She did not intend to show it, however.

'Look up there!'

It meant tilting her head back, which would hurt, and besides, it was like him to domineer even over where she should look!

'No! My whole face hurts!'

He caught her chin and forced her to look upwards, though she cried out at his touch and tears came to her eyes.

'I said look!'

Given no choice she obeyed him, then her eyes widened.

'Oh, Wolf, it's a man!'

He nodded grimly. 'That's right, a dead chief. The Indians in these parts bury their dead in the treetops to save them from marauding animals. A grave is a sacred thing, you see, and you were going to use it for target practice! Now do you see that when I give an order it has a good reason behind it?'

'But you didn't tell me not to shoot at it!'

He compressed his lips and sighed with exaggerated weariness.

'No, because you didn't announce your intention. But I struck the barrel up and you took the recoil in the face, which will probably make you think twice before firing at anything but a target when I'm with you.'

She glanced up again, seeing that the dead body had been disposed in a pre-natal position and wedged into a small coffin. The coffin had then been tilted, as if to give the dead man a view across the rolling grasslands. The chief was in his best clothing, with beads and bright feathers, looking dignified and patriarchal. And to think that she might have smashed a bullet right through that ancient, seamed forehead! She shuddered, then looked guiltily at Wolf.

'I'm sorry, truly.' Her voice was humble. 'I didn't know. And I've been well served, for my face does hurt.'

He led her out from the shadow of the trees into the sunlight on the bank. He took her face between both hands, the thumbs resting lightly beneath her chin, and began to feel the extent of the damage. She could not help flinching as his thumbs found and probed the swelling but she said nothing, closing her eyes so that he would not think the water which filled them was tears.

'Nothing broken, but there's a nasty lump on the jaw bone. Is the pain bad?'

His hands still framed her face. She opened her eyes and surprised an expression of rueful admiration in his gaze for a moment, but it shuttered at once, cold again.

'It hurts, but I'm sure it's nothing much.'

He released her, stepping back.

71

'Good. We'll finish off the target practice and get back to the others. I want to move on soon.'

Preceding him across the tree-trunk, she said: 'I can't shoot any more. My face is far too painful.'

They reached the place where he had leaned the gun against a tree and he picked it up, reloaded, then handed it to her.

'Six more shots, then we'll go back.'

She scarcely considered refusing for her head was aching violently and she had no desire to provoke another quarrel, particularly as it had not escaped her notice that he always won their encounters. She levelled the gun, cuddled the breech to her cheek, and fired. The tins scattered and to her surprise he took the gun from her, broke it, then went and retrieved the tins.

'That'll do for today. I'll show you how to clean the gun when we reach the camp.'

She plodded after him back to the camp, patiently cleaned the gun, then wearily mounted her mule once more. As they set out he rode alongside her, glancing down shrewdly at her white face with the bruise already darkening along her jaw.

'We're stopping at a missionary school tonight, with a small trading post. Perhaps I could get you a woman's saddle.'

'Could you do so?' She smiled lop-sidedly, recognizing an olive branch. 'And perhaps I could buy a riding skirt.'

By the time they reached their next camping place, however, she was so weary that she slid off the mule and just stood, wishing that she might lie down, but there was a meal to cook, unpacking to do, a fire to light... Leo came over to her, took the mule's reins, and advised her to lie down in the waggon.

'Oh Leo, I dare not! Wolf would...'

'But it was Wolf said you must rest, Miss.'

He heaved her into the waggon and she collapsed into her bedroll and slept like a log.

The next day was fine and though the bruise was livid the swelling on her jaw had gone down a little and Charlotte was no longer in pain. She got up, lit the fire and made breakfast, then left Leo to finish the chores since Wolf wanted to take her over to the trading post.

'We'll stay here tonight,' he told her as

73

he led her down a narrow dirt path with log cabins on either side. 'One of the waggon wheels split clean across yesterday, though it got us here. And I want Al Reynolds' bull to serve the dun cow; she's bulling.'

This was double-dutch to Charlotte, but she nodded sagely and saw his mouth quirk with unholy amusement.

'Do you know what I'm talking about?'

'No. But won't it be nice to stay in one place for a day or so!'

The largest of the log cabins was a mission school and directly abutting on to it was the store. Both buildings plainly formed the centre of the small community, but despite Charlotte's hopes neither side-saddle nor riding skirt was to be had. The missionary's wife, asked for advice by the dumpy, cross-eyed little squaw who helped to run the store, told her that so few women crossed by the plains route that there was no call for feminine fripperies. Charlotte could not consider a sidesaddle a 'feminine frippery', and rather resented the sidelong glances which the older woman kept shooting at her, especially since she was extremely friendly towards Wolf. If I'm a bad woman, then she ought to blame Wolf as well as me, she thought as they bade the woman goodbye and left the store. She voiced the thought aloud as they left the track and the little cluster of log cabins to return to the camp. Though the aforementioned articles had not been forthcoming, they had bought some supplies and Charlotte carried a gift from Wolf which she already valued—an Indian squaw's tunic, a knee-length garment made of soft-coloured doeskin, fringed at the hem and embroidered lavishly with brown, cream and orange-coloured wools. With this over her breeches, she need no longer feel quite so brazen, she told herself.

'If Mrs Reynolds thinks me no better than I should be, why is she so nice to you? I mean, if I *was* a bad woman, then I should need a man to be bad with me, should I not? I can scarcely be a bad woman on my own, can I? Have I got it right?'

'Yup. But Mrs Reynolds has seen me here a number of times, and knows I don't travel with a woman as a rule. I guess she thinks you've led me astray.'

Charlotte stopped dead in her tracks, eyes and mouth rounding.

'*Me?* She thinks I could lead you anywhere you didn't want to go? Why, she can't know you one little bit, or she would know you always do as you want to!'

'It's true you couldn't lead me any way I didn't want to go,' he acknowledged gravely, but devils danced in his narrowed eyes as he looked down at her. 'But who said I didn't want to be led astray?'

'Oh!' Her confusion was complete. 'But...but...'

He took pity on her, patting her shoulder. 'I think you'll find Mrs Reynolds will treat you more as an equal tomorrow morning. She'll keep an eye on us tonight, and when she sees you go into the waggon and the men go to their tents I guess she'll absolve you from being a bad woman.'

Charlotte sniffed and tossed her head. 'I don't care what she thinks. Stupid, narrow-minded woman, what difference does it make what she believes? When I'm living with Freddy in California I'll be every bit as respectable as her.'

They were passing through the trees which hid their encampment from the settlement and he stopped, catching her arm, pulling her to a halt. For a moment she quailed, fearing his wrath, but he only hushed her, pointing ahead.

Across the little glade which they were about to enter came a tiny fawn, trotting at its mother's heels, and because of Wolf's foresight they were able to enjoy an uninterrupted view of the creatures until they slipped into the trees. Charlotte sighed with pleasure.

'Weren't they lovely? And not a bit afraid.'

'They were upwind of us, so had no idea we were there. You run along now, I've still some business to attend to.'

They were on the outskirts of the camp, so she clutched the supplies to her bosom and hurried across to the fire to help Leo serve the meal. She was supposed to get the food with his assistance but because of Wolf's calls on her time it was often the other way around. To do him justice, Leo was the most willing helper and had no objection to cooking, provided he was told what to cook and how to cook it.

It was a good meal that night, for the store had sold them delicious smoked venison, potatoes and fat ears of maize, but rather to Charlotte's disappointment Wolf did not reappear and so missed the treat. Let him go hungry, if he's too superior to turn up at mealtimes, she told herself, with a crispness which scarcely went with the fact that she saved his portion in one of the saucepans, just in case he turned up late and hungry.

They were a happy party that night, for another waggon train had also made haste to arrive at the settlement, and the two groups gathered round the fire when their respective meals had been eaten, telling stories, singing songs, and passing round some beer which someone produced. In fact, Charlotte was the first one to make a move, when she thought she saw Wolf slipping through the shadows and into his own tent. Abruptly, all thought of staying up and offering to warm him up some food vanished; he was an ungrateful...

Sighing, she got up, bade the men goodnight, and climbed rather slowly into her cheese-smelling nest, though she was tired enough in all conscience. Her face ached a little too, a dull throbbing, and she told herself that she would sleep the sounder for having a late night. She could not help wondering why Wolf had absented himself from their gathering, then shrugged and took off the new Indian tunic. She reached out for her bedroll in the dark, not wanting to light a candle with the other waggon train so close, and something hit her in the face. Quite a small something, but it made her heartbeat quicken. She shook the bedroll and, as her eyes grew used to the dimness, saw small dark objects crawling and taking wing, buzzing and blundering round her head. Beetles! Hateful, horrible beetles!

Outside, the men were going off to their tents. Someone blundered into another man and there was jovial cursing and some laughter. She heard another man remark that 'some durned beetles' had got into his tent which he had left unlaced, but it sounded as though the majority of the men were untroubled, having had the good sense to leave their tents laced up. Charlotte, because of the cheeses always kept the flaps of the waggon well back so that the smell was less strong by the time she got to bed.

Now, she looked up at the canvas, then at the opening. She had a deep-rooted fear of all creepy-crawlies, and decided she would simply have to make a dash for it. She moved, and a beetle fell from the canvas overhead on to her shoulder.

She shrieked and cowered back against the end of the waggon where the cheeses reigned supreme. Suppose the creatures had fallen in her *hair?* It might happen at any moment, a beetle might fly on to her face.

'Help! Oh, Wolf, do come!'

Someone appeared in the gap at the end of the waggon, then she felt the vehicle lurch and saw him outlined against the night sky. He came unsteadily towards her, catching his foot in her blanket and muttering a curse.

'Miss Charlotte? Kin I help you, missie?'

It was the big redheaded man with the squint, Joab. She was immediately afraid. She had seen the way he watched her, his eyes gleaming with a greed she could not understand, his tongue licking his lips into fleshy, drooping redness.

'No, I was calling Wolf.' Then, when he still came on, she added boldly: 'Get out of my waggon!'

'Alone, missie?' He blundered nearer, his hands reaching out towards her. 'I thought you was alone, needin' a bit o' company.'

She was afraid of the beetles but more afraid of Joab. His eyes were still not used to the dimness, however—if she could slip past him, gain the open air...

He lurched against her and hands like beefsteaks grabbed and pawed at her shirt. She screamed breathlessly and he closed in on her, his face weaving in front of her own, his hot breath making her feel sick.

'C'mon, missie, no need to be shy with me! Seems Wolf don't want you, but there's them as do! Just let me...'

She scarcely noticed the waggon move as someone else climbed aboard until she heard Wolf's voice. Never had his harsh tones sounded sweeter!

'That's enough, Joab.'

His voice acted like a bucket of ice-cold water on her unwanted guest. He turned, offering a mumbled remark about too much whisky, the young lady being lonely. But Wolf merely caught him by the scruff of the neck and hurled him peremptorily out of the waggon. Charlotte heard the thud of a hard landing as she sagged weakly against the canvas and hoped viciously that Joab had broken every bone in his body. Then Wolf was beside her, tilting her face up to his, concern in his touch.

'Charlotte? You all right?'

She tried to answer, but her voice broke. He picked her up without more ado and carried her out of the waggon and into his own small tent. It was homely in there, with a candle wedged in a bottle casting a friendly glow on the bedding, the books, the paraphernalia he always had about him. He stood her up for a moment, then pushed her down to sit on his bedroll and squatted on his heels in front of her.

'He didn't hurt you? You're all right? Just shaken up?'

She nodded, then sniffed dolorously. It had been a nasty moment which but for Wolf's intervention would have been a great deal nastier, she fully appreciated that. Now reaction was setting in.

'I'm all right. But I h-hate him!'

He smoothed the damp hair off her brow, then patted her shoulder awkwardly.

'Poor Charlotte, I never should have let you sleep in that waggon. You'll sleep here in future.'

She blinked up at him, then fastened the top two buttons of her shirt, which she must have undone before Joab entered the waggon. 'I won't sleep in here. What's wrong with the waggon? He won't come back, will he?'

He leaned forward and touched her bruised jaw lightly, then his eyes flickered down to her fingers, busy on the shirt buttons. His nostrils flared.

'He would probably have raped you. Do you know that?'

She nodded, not looking at him.

'Look, the men thought you were my mistress, brought along for my own pleasure. They didn't resent it because I'm the trail boss, though no one else was allowed to bring a woman. But they must have watched, realized that I wasn't sleeping with you nor sneaking into the waggon in the course of the night, and they thought you were fair game. See?'

'But no one came near me before,' she objected. She stood up and he followed suit. 'Why was that, if they knew I wasn't your mistress?'

'Because until tonight I've always been around. No one was going to climb into that waggon and start anything with you in case I suddenly decided I wanted to visit you myself. But I was out tonight and Joab chanced his luck. If you're wise, you'll stay here.'

'And you? Will you sleep in the waggon?'

He laughed shortly. 'I shall not, but

neither shall I molest you. I've never cared for red-haired women.'

For a moment her hand itched to slap his face. Red-haired! She was *not* red-haired! Her hair was copper, and anyway he had shown no repugnance when he had kissed her down by the river. She knew the kiss had been a punishment for her slapping his face, but he had enjoyed it!

'It doesn't matter, because I'm going back to the waggon.'

To her secret surprise he made no effort to persuade her further, nor did he order her to remain. He simply shrugged and walked over to the tent flap. It was not laced up and he held it open politely.

'Very well, if that's what you want. Goodnight.'

She vouchsafed no answer but made her way back to the waggon. Climbing back in, she was very uneasy. Suppose Joab was lurking in the shadows, waiting to finish off what he had begun? She shuddered at the thought but forced herself to enter the gloom of the interior.

It was not he who waited. It was the beetles. What had brought them she could not imagine but they rose in a buzzing cloud as she entered, sending her leaping out of the waggon again and rushing back to Wolf's tent. He was sitting on his bedroll, grinning. He had stripped to his breeches and she saw that his chest was tanned and smooth except for a strong line of hair down the centre which widened as it met the waistband of his breeches. She dragged her eyes back to his face and saw he was watching her, obviously amused because she had never seen a man bare-chested before.

'Wolf, the waggon's full of beetles.'

'Is it?'

'Yes. Would you please come and scare them away.'

He got to his feet and walked past her and she followed him meekly back to the waggon. He climbed in and picked up her bedroll, then brought it outside and shook it vigorously. Bugs flew in all directions.

'Thank you,' Charlotte said humbly. 'And would you please knock down the ones on the canvas, so that I can sleep without being afraid they'll fall on me?'

But he had turned away and was making for his own tent, her bedroll still in his hand.

'No.'

She followed him, unable to believe her ears.

'You don't mean it! Well, if you won't scare them away I'll sleep under the waggon. Give me my bedding.'

'No.'

He went into his tent.

Irresolute, Charlotte walked back towards the waggon. Inside, bugs still whirred and crawled. She returned to the tent. She cleared her throat so he would know it was she, and entered.

'Wolf, I said I'd sleep under the waggon.'

He was laying her bedroll on the ground. He glanced up at her and indicated it with a jerk of the head.

'Get in.'

She crossed the tent with dragging steps. She was sure he would not harm her in any way, but it was not possible for her to share a tent with a *man!* Not even to let the other men believe her to be his woman!

'Why can't I sleep under the waggon? I'd be...'

'You'd be raped either by one of my men or by one of the men with the other waggon train,' he interrupted crisply. 'I

86

know these fellows, remember. Or is that what you want?'

She was tired and the insult implicit in the last question passed her by. She only knew that he was talking sense. If she spent the night in his tent, then the men would once again believe she was Wolf's woman, and she would be safe from them. She went over and climbed wearily into her bedroll, pulling the blanket up round her neck. Wolf came over and squatted beside her.

'Good girl.' She could hear the amusement in his voice. 'Now I'll stay here until I'm durned sure that everyone knows I'm in here, and then I'll share with Leo for the rest of the night.'

Tortoiselike, her head popped out of her bedroll. She beamed.

'Oh, Wolf! Oh, thank you! I'm sorry I thought...what did I think. I knew you wouldn't—I mean I just knew I'd be all right and that you wouldn't...'

He leaned over and doused the candle, then wagged an admonitory finger under her nose.

'Better stop now, before you say something you'll regret,' he advised her drily. 'Go to sleep!'

'I will, I will. I'm sorry I'm turning you out, though, making you share with Leo. I'm a nuisance, aren't I?'

'Yes, you are. And if you don't quit talking I'll come over there and make you stop. Think about your ruined reputation, that should shut your mouth for a bit.'

'What does it matter what the men think?' Charlotte murmured sleepily. 'They won't say anything.'

'No. But this'll give Mrs Reynolds food for thought!'

She groaned, then pulled the blanket up over her head. She heard him laugh, soft and deep in his throat, then he settled down by the unlaced opening of the tent, ready to slip away when the coast was clear. And much sooner than she had expected, she slept.

CHAPTER 4

In the days that followed the party covered difficult country where the cholera meant a grave every few yards, so that they looked forward to reaching Fort Laramie and having another taste of civilisation. It proved disappointing, however, since stocks had run very low, and though Wolf took Charlotte into the fort to try to purchase some warm clothing, they were unlucky. The only goods available were sacks of weevilly flour and old-fashioned mining equipment.

Moreover, there was an incident whilst they were camping near the Fort which reminded Charlotte sharply of a previous occasion. At their previous stop by a trading post, Wolf had gone off somewhere and Joab had attacked Charlotte. Now, she began to suspect where he had gone. There was an Indian encampment nearby and one of the squaws was very lovely, with a profile which reminded Charlotte of the head on a Greek coin and a magnificent figure obvious even beneath the long skin tunic and trousers that the squaws wore.

Twice, Charlotte surprised Wolf in conversation with the copper-skinned beauty and once he announced that he was going up to the Fort and would not allow her to accompany him, though she did ask if she might go. Worse, he was gone two whole hours and came back with such a smug expression on his handsome face that she could have hit him. It needed little imagination, she told herself furiously, to guess what he had been doing!

'Isn't it just like Wolf, to run around after a squaw though he's the one who said no women were to come on the expedition?' she said furiously to Leo as they prepared a meal one day. 'He's horrible if you and I laugh together, though he knows perfectly well we aren't carrying on! I'm disgusted and shan't have anything more to do with him.'

'Ain't you leapin' to conclusions?' Leo asked, grinning. 'Wolf's probably teachin' that squaw to shoot straight and mind her manners!'

'Huh! I know what he's teaching her, he's teaching her...' she paused, aware of the morass into which more plain speaking would lead her. 'Well, you know what I mean. Anyway, she won't need much teaching, I should think she knows it all already.'

'Well, it ain't none of our business,' Leo said easily, throwing pearl barley into the stew. 'You don't care what he gits up to with that li'l squaw, do you?'

'No, of course not,' Charlotte said hastily, realizing how her words could have been interpreted. 'He can make love with every Indian woman from here to California if it makes him happy! But if you or I behaved like he does, imagine what he'd say!'

They were alone in the camp since the men had gone to help another train whose waggons had stuck and swamped as they attempted the river crossing. The Cuban party, as Wolf's soldiers were called, were far too experienced to rush at a river and discover too late that it was deep or fast-running or soft-bottomed, but not everyone was so sensible. Wolf was not with the rescue party. He had returned to Fort Laramie, ostensibly to see if any stores had been delivered, though Charlotte supposed that he was really in the arms, of his Redskin charmer—not that she cared, of course, provided that he left her alone!

'Yeah, we've never behaved like he does,' Leo said thoughtfully. He turned to Charlotte. 'Though I can't imagine why not!'

Before she could think of a suitable reply, Leo had her in his arms and was planting puppyish and inexpert kisses on her cheeks, her eyelids, even on her mouth. She gasped and tried to push him away but he was stronger than she. He wrapped both arms round her and tipped her backwards, falling on top of her with enough force to knock all the breath out of her and still kissing her wildly.

Charlotte, wriggling desperately, shouted at Leo to get off but he took no notice and Charlotte suddenly had to fight an urge to giggle. He looked so red-faced and foolish, poor Leo, puffing and panting, trying to capture her mouth, too kind and naïve to grab her hair and hold her still as a less scrupulous man would have done.

It occurred to Charlotte at that point that she really was in a bad position. If the men came back from the river, what would they think?

'Leo! Attention!'

The abrupt, barking shout did in seconds all that Charlotte's wriggles and pleas had been unable to accomplish. Leo leapt off her as if stung and came raggedly to attention.

Charlotte, scrambling to her feet, saw Wolf standing, hands on hips, and waited for the heaven's to fall. He simply gave Leo a cold stare, however, and then beckoned to her.

'Here!'

Pushing her hair off her face, Charlotte followed, her cheeks burning. It was bad enough that Wolf had returned at such an inopportune moment, that he would now pretend to believe that she had encouraged Leo's advances, but what was worse was her inner knowledge that she had been a fool to allow Leo to misinterpret her friendliness to such an extent.

Wolf marched her over to where two waggons stood close enough to form a small enclosure and then faced her. He looked grim.

'Well? Bite off more'n you could chew?'

'No, it was just that we started talking about...' She remembered what they had been talking about and righteous indignation took the place of her sheepish, ashamed feeling. Why, if Wolf had not been carrying on with that squaw Leo would never have tried it on with her!

'About what? Moons and Junes?'

'No!' She snapped the word out, hating him for blaming her for something she could not help. 'Indian squaws, as it happens.' She waited for him to show some sign of guilt but he merely continued to look at her enquiringly. 'Some white men seem to think squaws are easy game,' she continued rather reluctantly. 'There was that girl at the Fort, the pretty one—she took your fancy, I could tell!'

'So you noticed?' He looked amused. 'I still don't see why that led Leo to pounce on you!'

'Don't you? Well, perhaps he felt that if other people could pounce on squaws, he could pounce on me!'

A dark brow rose lazily.

'You talk in riddles, Charlotte. Who's been pouncing on who, for the love of Mike? Give me a straight story, please.'

'I have given you a straight story!' She was so cross at his deliberate obtuseness that she stamped her foot. 'You went off with that squaw and no one's allowed to say anything!'

'*Leo* remarked on my going off with the squaw? *Leo* said I should be told off?'

As usual, he seemed to have driven her into a corner. She felt her cheeks begin to burn all over again and heard herself begin to stammer.

'N-no, not exactly. It was m-me who noticed the squaw, and I said...' She risked a peep up at him and decided against repeating her actual words; he looked dangerous suddenly, and very large. 'I said you'd gone off alone with the squaw, but you wouldn't be made to feel small because of it.'

'Oh, yeah? That was all? Well now, I wonder what I ought to do to you this time, Charlotte? Seems to me if I leave you for five minutes you're into mischief of one sort or another. First you get Joab into the waggon to kill beetles and dam' near get raped instead, now I find you with another guy on top of you! I suppose you'll say it was just horseplay?'

'I don't know precisely what horseplay is,' Charlotte said, looking hopefully up into his face. 'But Leo meant nothing; can't we forget it?'

'What about Leo? Can he forget it? Kissing's easier to start than to stop.'

The undoubted truth of this statement made Charlotte's mouth droop. She knew that the feeling of Wolf's mouth on hers would haunt her till her dying day.

'Yes, I know, but I'll speak to him. I'll tell him we can't be friends if he behaves like that again.'

'Right.' He caught her shoulders and swung her round towards the camp fire, then gave her a shove. 'Tell him right now!'

She threw a look of black dislike over her shoulder, making him chuckle.

'No need to push! And just you stay away until it's over!'

If Wolf had planned it, he could not have thought of a better way to make Leo and Charlotte more constrained in each other's company. For days they behaved almost like strangers, ill at ease over their cooking pots and unable to act naturally.

However, she had cause to be grateful to Wolf. When they had left Fort Laramie behind and were in the foothills of the Black Hills, Wolf came over to her one morning before they struck camp. She was sitting on her bedroll in the tent entrance, spreading lotion over her insect bites, and he stood for a moment grinning down at her, his arms full of what looked like an animal.

'Want any help? I'd be glad to assist.'

'No!' snapped Charlotte, putting the lid back on the bottle of lotion. Damn the man, why did he always catch her at awkward moments?

'Right. Catch!'

The animal suddenly came flying through the air towards her. Charlotte caught it by a reflex action and then gave a cry of pleasure. It was a cloak made from animal fur, with the soft side against her skin and the leather outside so that the water would run off it. She put it round her shoulders and it felt beautifully warm and comforting.

'Thank you—it's lovely! What is it?'

'Pine marten, I think. Glad you like it.'

He was halfway out of the tent when she remembered something.

'What do I owe you for this?'

'Nothing. It's a present.'

This was coals of fire indeed! She said humbly, 'Thanks again,' and then, as it occurred to her: 'Did the store re-stock, then? I suppose they didn't have any carrots or coffee?'

'Nope. Got it from a trapper. Best get movin', we leave in ten minutes.'

The trek from Fort Laramie through the Black Hills was both long and hard and took the Cuban Company eleven days of almost uninterrupted journeying, though they made camp each night. There were incidents, of course—Tallis was thrown from his mule and sustained a bruised posterior which caused great amusement, they stopped one day by a river because the grazing was good and found themselves surrounded by rattlesnakes—and Leo and Charlotte began to resume their former easy relationship.

Leo was the first to break the ice. He rode up beside her as she was making the best speed she could towards a new camping place and put a tentative hand on Tandy's bridle.

'Hold on a moment, Charlotte. I wanna say...you still mad at me?'

'Oh, Leo, of course not!' She laughed, turning to him. 'It was embarrassing for both of us, but now we'll be friends and forget the other business, shall we?'

'I reckon. I did feel kinda foolish.'

As if their renewed friendship had actually shortened the trail, they hit the foothills next day, and were soon heading for Fort Hall.

'A real store,' Charlotte said dreamily, gazing at the rough track between Tandy's pricked ears. 'With pats of butter, new baked bread, honey, jam...and, jars of sweets and chocolates, and fruit cordials, and...'

'Hold hard, I'm dribblin',' Leo said

crossly. 'I crave candies!'

'I do, because we're so low on sugar,' Charlotte confessed. 'I wonder whether I might get another set of clothes? My shirt's getting really nasty and I've not changed my breeches since I got them!'

'I doubt they'll have clothes,' Leo said. 'But wait and see's best, hey?'

Charlotte did get her change of clothing, though in a way which went to her heart.

A few days later they came to a bad river crossing, where the water ran fast and deep, and having tried it and realized that it was not suitable for the waggons to cross, Wolf sent the drivers round by a more circuitous route though he said that riders, if they wished, might swim their mounts across.

Charlotte, looking at the apparent depth of the water, was doubtful if she and Tandy could make it, but on the other hand the thought of riding behind the waggons on a trail which was further round and, according to Wolf, deep in mud, did not much appeal. In the end, she decided to take her chance in the water, even though she could not swim.

'I'll keep an eye on you,' Wolf said when

he saw her shivering on the bank. 'Don't worry, just hang onto Tandy's saddle and you'll be fine.'

It was a frightening experience, nevertheless. All the while Tandy was crossing Charlotte could feel the tug of the current against her legs and the coldness of the water numbed her quite quickly, which was also frightening. But she and the mule stumbled out on the opposite bank, to a cheer from two or three young men from another waggon train who had also chosen this route.

They seemed to be arguing, Charlotte noticed as she began to wring out as much of her shirt as she could. But then there was a splash and a halloo, and the first of the young men was in, swimming strongly for the bank. A moment later the second jumped and then the third, and despite herself, Charlotte lingered to watch them safe ashore.

The first two made it easily but the third was only a stripling of perhaps fifteen, and he was struggling. The first boy across gave a cry and Wolf, taking in the situation at a glance, ran down to the water's edge and began to wade in.

They had gone under, but Wolf and the

older lad managed to reach him and to bring him out on to the bank. After a few minutes' attempted resuscitation, however, Wolf stood up again, shaking his head, his chest heaving from his exertions.

'No good.' He turned to the two older boys and it was obvious, now, that they were brothers. 'I'm sorry, he's gone.'

It was a very subdued party of riders which took the boys round with them to where they would meet their parents' waggon train. They carried the body of their younger brother wrapped in a piece of canvas, and Charlotte heard the mother's shocked scream followed by a long, agonised moaning and weeping as the boys told her the dreadful news.

They did not remain long with the mourners, having ascertained that they had the means to bury their dead and to erect a cross with a name carved on it, over the grave, but rode on to join their own vehicles, all of them saddened and shocked by the tragedy.

So when, next day, Wolf appeared in the doorway of the chuck waggon where Charlotte was preparing to cook the noon meal and handed her two checked shirts and another pair of breeches, Charlotte was at a loss to know where he had got them.

'Well, thank you,' she said doubtfully. 'Did you ride ahead to Fort Hall and buy them there? Otherwise I can't imagine...'

'Nope. Got them from another train,' Wolf said briefly. 'Try 'em on for size.'

'Another train?' Charlotte frowned. 'B-but didn't the fellow need them? People don't usually bring clothes they aren't going to need!'

'He won't be wanting them again.'

She looked up, into Wolf's face, and knew where the clothing had come from. It had belonged to that poor young boy, drowned at Thomas's Fork! She thrust the clothing wildly away from her, staring indignantly up at Wolf.

'No! It's the drowned boy's, isn't it? You're hateful, Wolf, hateful!'

Quite calmly, he picked up the clothes and handed them back to her. She let them fall. Once more he bent and picked up the garments.

'Why am I hateful? D'you think the boy 'ud grudge his clothes being used? D'you think his mother would have passed them on—she wouldn't accept any payment, only I gave the older boy a hunting knife—d'you think she'd have passed them on gladly if she thought they'd be scorned? If that's a sample of your English manners...'

Silently Charlotte took the clothes from him. She turned her back on her work and went over to where a pile of barrels would hide her from view and began to change. Presently she emerged in the new garments.

'I'm sorry, it was rude and foolish of me. Thank you very much, Wolf, they fit f-fine.'

She was very near tears and for once he was understanding, though he said little more. But there was no harshness in the hand that tipped her face up to his and even smiled slightly.

'Good girl.'

No one commented on Charlotte's sudden acquisition of a change of clothing, and Charlotte realized that it was probably because no one noticed. The men mostly had a change of garment, but since they all seemed to wear checked shirts and dun-coloured breeches they could have worn the same pair for months together without anyone being any the wiser. Only she, desperately trying to launder their mired and stained clothing, knew that they did, from time to time, indulge themselves with a change of shirt and breeches.

At Fort Hall, a great many of their deficiencies, or at least the deficiencies of the chuck waggon, were made good. Flour, sugar and coffee were here, on the neat little shelves in the food store, as well as a big clay jar of wild bees' honey, a quantity of very good butter and some of the rice and root vegetables which Charlotte had come to rely on so heavily when she was preparing a meal.

They all liked Fort Hall. It was an efficient and well-run place, handsome, too. Made of adobe and wood, it was built round a square central courtyard, in the middle of which a fountain played, and the ground floor of the building consisted of perhaps a dozen small rooms, each one specializing in something different, so that at one window you could buy dry goods, at another cereals, and at another still farming implements and saddlery.

Above, on the first floor, was the apartment of the man who ran the Fort for the Hudson Bay Fur Company, a certain Captain Grant. He impressed all the Cuban party with his kindly and helpful attitude and also by the efficiency with which he ran his business. Not like Fort Laramie, where the proprietor seemed to want neither to buy nor to sell.

As most of the trail bosses had done, Wolf had stocked up in St Joe's with a number of things which he did not particularly want, but which he hoped would be needed along the route, and it seemed he had more than a few shillings. Some of the things he purchased were to cause Charlotte several headaches, though she was still in ignorance of this when Wolf stalked into the encampment one afternoon with the news that he needed a calm, placid mule to help bring back his purchases.

'Tandy's pretty good,' Charlotte said, all unsuspecting. 'Shall I saddle her up?'

'No. I'll take her, though. I'll rope the crates to her back; it isn't a long journey.'

'What've you bought?' Charlotte demanded, insatiably curious. 'Something nice? A whole crate of...of...not oranges?'

'That's right. Not oranges.' He relented at her moan and grinned. 'Chickens. Hens, I should say. They're in lay. Oh, and a goat with a kid at heel. You'll like 'em.'

'I shan't have to like them,' Charlotte said. 'They're nothing to do with me, you bought them!'

He chuckled and tipped his hat down over his nose so that he had to put his head back to look down at her, then he caught her shoulder and swung her round to face him just as she was about to move away.

'Nothing to do with you? You're the cook! Cook always takes care of livestock.'

'The only thing I do with livestock,' Charlotte said coldly, 'is cook it. I *won't...*'

'You will, Charlotte.'

And that, of course, was the end of the argument, though not of Charlotte's silent rebellion. She rebelled as soon as she saw the chickens, horrid, scrawny little things, ruffled and untidy with a tendency to peck each other's feathers out. And the goat was worse, the goat was a horrid, smelly black one with yellow eyes and tiny sharp horns. Her name, Wolf informed Charlotte blandly, was Emily and the kid was Sally, and she must learn to milk the one and love the other.

She looked *I won't* at him, but knew that it was hopeless. She might never learn to love any of her new charges, but she was very sure that Wolf would see she learned to take care of them!

'We'll have a rest day, here,' Wolf announced when they reached a pleasant spot not too far from the falls on Snake River. They had passed the big American falls some time previously, and Charlotte had marvelled at the tremendous swoop and crash of the water as it fell thirty feet into the gorge below, sounding so loud that it had formed a background to their journey all the previous day. But the falls gradually grew fewer and smaller, and now the river was placid enough and their camp was shaded from the sun by a clump of fine, tall pine trees. Grass grew in abundance upon the bluffs which rose from the river, and it seemed in every way a good place to camp, especially as Wolf had announced that he'd seen sizeable fish when he watered Stormbird earlier.

For some reason, they had been having very hot weather at last, and pleasant though it was to have constant sunshine it was not so pleasant to have to face the clouds of suffocating dust raised by the waggons. So a rest day was doubly welcome to them all and Charlotte, secure in the knowledge of a chuck waggon well filled with good things, was delighted at the chance of a break.

'Would it be possible for me to have a bathe, do you think?' she said shyly to Wolf, when the men had eaten their evening meal and were yarning and drinking round the fire. 'Perhaps if I made the noon meal and then went down when everyone was eating...?'

'Guess so. I'll see to it.'

And next day he was as good as his word. After breakfast various ploys were undertaken by the men, including the gargantuan one of breaking up a waggon in order to use the spare parts thus gained to mend the remaining roadworthy ones. Since this also meant that a mule-team would be going spare, the teamsters were delighted and helped to dismember the oldest and least reliable waggon with a good deal of enthusiasm.

This task was still not completed at noon, but Charlotte was serving roast chicken, so everyone crowded round the campfire. They were not her own much disliked hens but prairie chickens, and made very good eating. She served everyone, then looked hopefully across at Wolf, who nodded and got to his feet.

'Here a moment, Charlotte.'

He led her down to the river and along it a short way, to where a pool, both deep and beautiful, was charged and recharged by a tumbling waterfall. Charlotte smiled delightedly and laid her towel over the nearest bushes.

'This is wonderful—thank you, Wolf! May I go in now?'

'Yup. Rinse under the fall. I'll be over there.'

Charlotte accordingly soaped herself, stood under the fall and rinsed off the soap again and then made for the bank once more, where she dried, dressed, and then returned to the camp with Wolf, chattering away to him in a friendly fashion. A rest day did wonders for everyone's temper!

During the afternoon she played a ridiculous game with a ball and homemade bats which Johnnie Tillett had invented and which he played with a good deal of skill, then she cooked a huge suet pudding with treacle sauce, and finally, after a quiet evening darning socks, she went to bed rested and happy with her day.

It was strange, then, that after such a

good day the following one should be so bad. It even began badly.

They hit the trail under a bright sun, then struck a marshy patch where mosquitoes the size of fruit bats attacked them relentlessly, and even when they left the mosquitoes behind (they only seemed the size of fruit bats, Charlotte admitted when Leo queried her eyesight) the trail was difficult and tempers frayed easily.

When they stopped to eat, Wolf decided that it would be easier on everyone if they remained at this spot, had a nap, and then left again in the cool of the evening, so Charlotte lit the fire under her camp oven and prepared to bake bread.

Wolf had been short-tempered since the last meal and Charlotte, seeing Mr Hobbs hovering, gave him a griddle cake sprinkled with sugar and asked what was wrong with the team boss.

'Seems some Injuns got two white men yesterday,' he said in answer to her question. 'Wandered off from the waggons, sightseeing like, and got took. Them braves tortured 'em so bad that though the party paid the ransom one of 'em died this morning.'

'Gosh,' Charlotte said feelingly. 'No wonder Wolf's in such a foul temper—did you hear him telling the fellow who's shoeing the mules that he could do a better job himself?'

Leo, listening, chuckled.

'Did you hear him tell me I hadn't got the sense of a mule, just acos I moved a barrel of lard and cracked some eggs?'

'No, I didn't, but I can see we'll have to handle Wolf with kid gloves for today.'

Charlotte really meant to do so, realizing how upset the team boss must have been when he visited the train up the trail and heard their news, but unfortunately that very afternoon, her temper got the better of her again.

It was all the bread's fault. She had had so many perfect bakings, but this one just would not go right. The dough did not rise when it was set near the fire to prove, when she wanted more milk for the mixture she found it had turned sour and finally, when at last the loaves seemed fit for the oven, the wretched thing had managed to cool too much so that the bread just sat there,

111

uncooked and uncooking, whilst Charlotte fumed.

Into this culinary disaster area Wolf blew like a hurricane.

'Look at you, woman, mooning about here! That damned goat's got loose and she's eaten one of my socks—the one you were *supposed* to be darning. Get a move on, will you? I want this meal eaten in an hour!'

Charlotte, already hot and furious, jumped to her feet. She had known no swearwords when she left Liverpool, but she had culled a few on the immigrant ship, a few more in New York, and since she joined the Cuban party her vocabulary had increased quite fast. Now she used some of her worst words, spitting them at Wolf with all the annoyance that she had been bottling up over the bread, and finished by screaming at him that he could cook the bloody meal himself. Then, in a flood of tears, she would have gone and flung herself down in the cheese waggon, where she frequently lurked before her tent was erected, particularly now that the cheeses were no more, except that Wolf pursued her, grabbed her, and dragged her across his knee.

'If you ever swear at me again I'll tan your hide off you,' he said breathlessly, beginning to spank. 'I said the meal was to be served at once, I didn't say I wanted your opinion of me!'

'Let me go, you swine, you pig, you blockhead,' Charlotte shrieked, kicking and biting for all she was worth. 'I hate you, I hate you, I hate you! Let me go or I'll kill you!'

'No you won't, not by the time I've finished with you you won't,' Wolf said, grimly spanking. 'You'll apologize to me, that's what you'll do.'

But when he eventually let her go, suppressing the cries of pain he ought to have uttered when her teeth nearly met in his thigh, she simply screamed a couple more choice phrases at him and disappeared at a fast run behind the waggons.

He followed, of course. But he did not appreciate the extent of her rage and humiliation. She was sure that every man in the camp had been watching him spank her. He had made her look a fool, and she hated him. She would not stay here to be treated like that, she would go away and find another waggon train. She was a good cook now; anyone would be glad to have her work for them!

Accordingly, instead of hiding amongst the waggons as Wolf assumed she would, she wriggled under one of them and out the other side, and then made with all speed for the shelter of a clump of pines which grew at the foot of one of the bluffs which backed the valley.

It did not take her more than a few moments to gain the summit where she lay down, on her stomach for obvious reasons, and simmered, planning elaborate revenges on Wolf and thinking how she would tell her new team boss all about him and pour scorn on his absent head.

For ten minutes she watched Wolf search for her, and then he gave up. She guessed he thought she was inside one of the waggons, hiding, and knew it would take him a good half hour just to check each one thoroughly. He had said he wanted the evening meal eaten in an hour and he must realize that in her present mood she was unlikely to turn round and cook it. Leo and the rest of the men were fishing, so at least her spanking had been a private affair, but even so Wolf would either have to do something about the meal or get the men back from their fishing to do it for him.

She watched with considerable glee as he began to peel swedes. Serve him right, do him good! Her temper had cooled considerably by this time and she had no intention of running away, finding another waggon train. After all, Wolf was the only man who knew how she had been treated and she would find some way to teach him not to do it again, apart from biting his thigh!

He turned from the fire, absently rubbing his leg, and Charlotte, chuckled to herself, then saw him begin to build up the fire with dry wood and buffalo chips which she had put near it for that purpose. He opened her oven and saw the bread, nicely cooked by the look of it, and tried to get it out without using the cloth. Charlotte chuckled again as he drew back quickly, blowing on his fingertips.

It was then that she saw, out of the corner of her eye, the tiniest of tiny movements. She glanced sideways, and suppressed a gasp. Lying not more than six feet from her was an Indian brave, copper-skinned and wearing only moccasins and a pair of doeskin trousers, with yellow and blue stripes painted across his chest and upper arms. He was staring down into the camp, concentrating so fiercely that he had never even noticed her lying near him in the long grass!

She dared not move, for she could see that he had a rifle, though it was only lying beside him at the moment. Then she saw that he was not looking down into the camp, but at something nearer. She followed his gaze, and realized what it was.

Stormbird, head raised, delicate ears pricked forward, was coming up the hill towards them. Once he stopped, and at once the Indian made an odd, whinnying sound which brought the horse moving forward once more.

At once, Charlotte realized what was happening. Indians were notorious horse-traders, and notorious horse-thieves, too. This brave had seen Stormbird and coveted him, and was now luring him up the hill until he could get him close enough to grab.

Then Charlotte heard a tiny movement

behind the brave, and her heart nearly stopped. Was she wrong, was it a war party?

But it was the Indian's mare, lying absolutely flat and still in the grass, and Charlotte realized something else. There were other horses grazing down there, yet only Stormbird was showing any interest in the Indian and his mare because he was the only stallion in the Cuban party's stock. The mare was bait!

It was at this point that she looked beyond Stormbird, and saw that Wolf was following his horse. He was coming fast, his eyes fixed on Stormbird, plainly intending to see what was fascinating the animal.

The Indian suddenly saw him as well. He came up on his elbows and reached for the rifle and...God, he was pointing the barrel straight at Wolf's heart!

She had no choice, and in that moment Charlotte knew it. She jumped to her feet, screamed like a steam train, and then bounded across the short distance between them and hit the Indian squarely in the chest, collapsing on top of him, knocking the rifle out of his hands and effectively squashing him.

But it did not stop him. His arms crushed round her and he lifted her up, gave that odd, whinnying cry again, and then she felt him mount his mare with her still held captive in his arms. She was crushed against a sweaty, painted chest and knew that he was using her body as a shield so that Wolf would not fire—knew, too, that he was laughing, which struck her as very strange. She had not thought of an Indian having a sense of humour, being amused! For a moment she hoped that this was just a dream or a mad prank—perhaps the man was just dressed and painted like an Indian, perhaps he was really someone quite ordinary! But she knew in her heart that this was real and earnest. She struggled as the mare began to pick up speed, hoping to drop to the ground so that Wolf could rescue her, but the Indian only gripped her harder, and presently she felt him reach for the rifle which had been digging into her side. She looked up just as he reversed it and brought the butt down, hard, against her head.

After that, she knew nothing. She never felt herself slung across the saddle like a dead deer, nor counted the miles as they fled by beneath the mare's neat hooves.

CHAPTER 5

'I followed all right, but I was too far behind—it wasn't easy to catch Stormbird, he was upset by the whole business—and the mare soon had him out of sight.' Wolf, regaling Leo with the story as far as he knew it, chuckled. 'My, you should have seen Charlotte, though, fighting like a little tigress until he clubbed her over the head.'

'Hey, he didn't kill her?' Leo's freckled face paled.

'No, he'll likely want her for a ransom or something.' Wolf was packing two saddlebags with speed and despatch. 'Look, I'm going after her but I don't want the whole train held back. Will you press on, Leo, and boss the party for me? Take 'em through to just before the Humboldt Sink. We'll catch you up there.'

'I'll do my best, Wolf. But what if...well, say you ain't through findin' her by the time we git to the Sink?'

'Wait a day, then go on,' Wolf decided.

He filled a flask with brandy, then buckled the saddlebag. 'Here, get me some food and I'll be off.'

'Right. I made hash outa jerked beef. That do you?'

'Fine. Now look, they'll want a ransom, or they may do, but I can't trail a selection of goods about with me like some damned trader. If I send someone with a message, red or white, Leo, see that they get what they come for.' He paused. 'She's a good little cook,' he said with seeming irrelevance. 'Besides, I don't aim to reach California one short.'

'Could I come with you?' Leo asked eagerly. 'I could help you, you could send me back for the ransom if...when you find her.'

'Nope. Don't worry, feller, I'll find her.'

Presently, his saddlebags heavy with necessities, Wolf mounted Stormbird and set off at the lazy, deceptively slow canter with which his stallion ate up the miles.

He had told Leo not to worry, but he scarcely dared to let his mind dwell on what might happen to Charlotte. He had seen the man who had been taken and tortured by the Indians, and understood the reasoning behind it which seemed so twisted to European minds. Courage was all-important, so the braves had scourged the two white men with whips until their backs were bloodied pulp because they wanted to see if white men had courage as the red man had. And when the white men cried out and cringed under the lash, the braves felt superior. Suppose they hurt Charlotte? A mental picture of her agonies was foolish, because Indians respected women, or rather they thought of them as a man's right, not a man's enemy. They would not hesitate to take a white woman to wife, if she pleased them. He found this thought only slightly pleasanter than the thought of her being scourged, but at least such a marriage would mean nothing in European eyes. Nevertheless, he prayed he would reach her soon.

Charlotte came to herself to find someone trickling water on to her face and making cooing noises. She opened her eyes to find herself lying on a river bank, with the brave hanging over her. When he saw that she was awake he gave a grunt of satisfaction and pulled her to a sitting position, then up to her feet. He indicated the mare, cropping the grass a few feet away, and then tapped the butt of his rifle, an unmistakable question in his eyes.

Charlotte quickly tried to indicate that she would not try to escape again. She had no wish for a second knock-out blow with her head still ringing from the first one!

So it was with some degree of dignity that she and her captor rode into the Indian's village later that same day. It was in a deep, dark pine forest, though she saw that ahead the trees were no more than a thick belt, with the long grass of the prairie beyond them. Her heart sank. It was a good place to hide, the sort of place that might not be found in a hundred years of searching.

This was quite a big village with upwards of a dozen wigwams or leather lodges scattered round the edge of it. They were painted in white and scarlet and were made of buffalo skins, cunningly draped over pine-poles to give them the conical shape she saw. There were other wigwams too, smaller ones, and in the centre of the clearing a number of women were working, looking similar in a way to any country women working anywhere. Gossiping, laughing, admiring each other's work.

Her captor lifted her off the mare and took her upper arm. He made no attempt to take the horse off to rub it down or feed it, but a woman detached herself from the group and came towards the mare, taking it by its rope bridle and leading it over to where other horses grazed. But Charlotte did not have time to see what happened next for her captor strode into one of the bigger wigwams, dragging her after him.

For a moment she could see nothing. Then she saw...eyes! Wherever she looked it seemed that there were eyes, white-rimmed with surprise, staring at her. Then she saw smiles, gleaming white teeth. She stared hard into the gloom. It looked like a gathering of elderly men—she could see no women—but there was a foetid animal stench which was making her eyes water, as did the smoke from the open fire. Some of the smoke went out through the circular opening in the top of the wigwam, but a good deal lingered still, making the air thick and blue.

Her captor pulled her forward so that she stood near enough to the fire for the flames to illumine her features. He held her firmly, with one hand round both her wrists, which were twisted behind her back. He did not want to hurt her, she was sure, but merely to show her off to these old men—if they were old men.

She could hear them talking among themselves, studying her curiously, even more so when her captor loosed her hair and the shining flood of coppery-red gleamed in the firelight. There was a murmur, whether of appreciation or repulsion she could not tell and did not much care, except that she found herself hoping her hair would be allowed to remain on her scalp and would not end up decorating some squaw's deerskin belt!

She was still standing there, her eyes going from face to face, when it occurred to her that her captor seemed to be making a request or suggestion of some sort and that the elderly men round the fire were concurring. At least, they were grunting, which probably meant much the same thing in any language. When all the grunting had ceased the brave took her out of the wigwam once more and hurried her across the clearing, blinking in the suddenly bright light. They went into another wigwam, but this time the smell was less strong and there was less smoke as well. A child toddled across her path, looking up to smile into her face with that artless, innocent smile which all children under three possess as of right. She smiled back, and was then pushed almost into the arms of another Indian—a squaw this time, with a broad, rather cow-like face and a baby at her hip. The brave spoke briefly, the woman took Charlotte's arm, and then the brave turned and disappeared.

At once, the woman took Charlotte over to a bed or couch made of animal skins and sat down upon it, indicating that Charlotte was to follow suit. Charlotte did so and the woman untied a thong at the front of her dress to reveal a large, coffee-coloured breast. She put the baby to it and, once it was feeding, patted her other breast.

'Ahabi. Ahabi.'

It was plain that this was her name. Charlotte, in her turn, touched her own breast.

'Charlotte. I am Charlotte.'

They smiled at one another. It was a start at least, an attempt to get to know one another, and Charlotte was determined to get through to these people, for how else could she persuade them to go back to the waggon train and ask for a ransom? She never doubted for a moment that Wolf would pay a ransom for her, little though he might want to, because he was honourable, in his way, and would not leave her here, amongst an alien race, not speaking the language, not understanding anything about the people or their customs.

She just hoped that someone would learn to talk to her soon!

It took Charlotte only a few hours of intensive watching and making guesses by sign language to realize what was in the wind. Chapaupau, the brave who had captured her, was married not only to Ahabi but also to Singueapech and Tollamea, and it was his intention to add Charlotte to his string of women. Ahabi explained by signs, that the three women and their children lived happily together in this big wigwam and that sometimes Chapaupau would come and take one of them away with him, to his smaller wigwam on the men's side of the clearing. She made it plain that this was the ideal way of life, with three women sharing the cooking, cleaning and child-rearing whilst in return their husband fed them, cared for them and gave them babies.

'Why me? Why should he want to marry me?' Charlotte said, in the language of the flickering hand and expressive eyes, and the answer seemed to be 'Because you are beautiful, strong, and most important of high courage'. Ahabi, with much laughter, told the story, in pantomime, of how Charlotte had saved Wolf by springing like a prairie wolf upon their lord and master. The other two wives, both a good deal younger and prettier than Ahabi, laughed too, but admiringly, and told Charlotte, also in pantomime, that she would bear their lord many strong sons.

At least, she told herself that this was what they meant, though there could have been other, less happy, interpretations!

'Wolf is my man,' Charlotte said over and over again, trying to explain to them why she had fought their lord. They understood, but asked whether she had babies by him and, when she shook her head, indicated that no man owned a woman save by possessing her. Since she was not possessed by this Wolf, then

127

she was free to take Chapaupau for her husband.

To shout 'But I don't want Chapaupau' would not have gone down well, so Charlotte merely contented herself when they said this by sighing and casting her eyes up at the top of the wigwam in a very speaking way. She had no intention of giving up gracefully and sinking without a fight into the Indian's strong-smelling embrace!

That first night the women spread the skins out in front of the fire and pulled her down with them so that they might sleep around her. At first, Charlotte waited in fear and trembling in case Chapaupau decided to come and winkle her out for his pleasure that very night, for she was determined to sell her virtues dear and to fight every inch of the way to her bridal bed. But the night wore on, the squaws snored, the dogs crept in from the outer darkness and snored too, fleas hopped off the dogs—or possibly off the squaws—and made Charlotte's lot hideous, and she decided that she might as well run for it right now, before a fate worse than death overtook her. She did not, in fact, consider it a fate worse than death, but with Chapaupau it would be no picnic, and anyway she was spoken for; Wolf had said so!

She got up as silently as she could and stole towards the dim light showing at the entrance. If someone woke she would say that she was answering a call of nature which would puzzle them, since she had a suspicion that the squaws were not above using a corner of the wigwam for that purpose if they did not wish to go outside. Certainly there was a very strong, eye-watering odour where the buffalo skin was pegged down to the right of the entrance.

It was as well that her nerves were strong for lying right across the threshold was a man; in the dim, pre-dawn light it was impossible to say for certain who it was, but she supposed it must be Chapaupau. She hesitated, but he seemed fathoms deep in sleep so she stepped over him, and had one foot on the right of him and the other on the left when she felt her ankles caught in a grip of iron.

Some women might have screamed, but Charlotte was far too angry with herself to show such a sign of weakness. Instead, as she fell, she lashed out with her fist, landing her would-be husband a terrific punch on the nose. She fell heavily, too, and for a moment the two of them lay eye to eye and breast to breast, the one's eyes watering from a punched nose, the other's from the violence of her fall. For a moment she thought she read retaliation in those dark, enigmatic eyes but then he grunted, got to his knees, dragged her to hers and pushed her back into the wigwam. She turned her head and looked into his face and read the message there—no hitting, no telling tales, but a plain order for all that not a word had been said. Go back, lie down, and you won't be punished. But give me any more trouble and I'll make you regret it.

Sighing with frustration and aching with the shock of her fall, Charlotte went meekly back and lay down amongst the squaws, the furs and the fleas.

In daylight, Charlotte was able to take a better look at the wigwam where she had spent the night. It certainly housed a good many things other than the Indians for it was here that Chapaupau kept his fishing spears, his tall bow and a supply of arrows, a child-sized canoe and paddle and various game bags and implements to which Charlotte could not put a name. There was also a manger with corn in it and Ahabi managed to convey to her that in winter, when it was truly cold, the horses and cattle would also be brought into the wigwam.

Thanking heaven that it was still only July, Charlotte asked a few more questions about tribal ceremonies, and learned that there would be a ceremony of some description before her husband would be allowed to get her with papoose. That was comforting, as was the fact that Ahabi managed to tell her some of the village elders thought Chapaupau was making a big mistake. Why this was so she found out when the sun was high in the sky and a stranger wandered into the village.

She, Ahabi and Tollamea were sitting before the big central fire in the clearing, roasting pieces of meat for the children who clustered round hopefully, when Ahabi jumped to her feet and said clearly, in passable French: 'Aha, c'est M Robinaux! C'est bien!'

For one incredulous moment, Charlotte just stared. Surely it was not possible that this good-natured, placid woman spoke

French, that all this time they had been struggling with sign language because it had never occurred to either of them that they had a language in common?

'What did you say, Ahabi?' she said casually, also in French. 'Who is the gentleman?'

'C'est M Robinaux,' Ahabi said instantly, adding, in French, 'He trader, he good man.'

The man was tall with shoulder-length ringlets and a skin quite dark enough, from a distance, to confuse him with the Indians, but he greeted Charlotte in impeccable and rapid French.

'My dear child, how came you here?'

Charlotte jumped to her feet and would have approached him, but he waved her back.

'No, no, don't let us annoy anyone. I understand that you're the girl Chapaupau intends to make his fourth wife?'

'Well, yes, but I'm sure my friends will pay a handsome sum of money for my safe return,' Charlotte said eagerly. 'I've been hoping that someone would find me, take a message back to the Cuban party, who are on the trail to California. I suppose...could you...?'

'The Cuban party. Why are they called that, pray?'

'Because they were all soldiers who fought in the Spanish—American war in Cuba. The trail boss is called Wolf.'

'Aha.' He was eyeing her curiously. 'And you, my dear, came with these soldiers?'

Charlotte felt her cheeks grow hot.

'I have to get to California so I'm working my passage as cook,' she explained. To her relief he nodded.

'I see. Well, I'm a fur trader and I visit a good many Indian villages to buy their furs so I'm well-known and frequently sought for information about the tribes. I think your brave will relinquish you for a ransom, partly because the elders wish him to do so. You see, the elders would all enjoy a share of the ransom, all the tribe would be enriched by it, but Chapaupau is the only one who would enjoy the—the benefits of a white bride. And of course they do know that there are white men who would take exception to a redskin's taking a girl by force.'

Charlotte sighed deeply.

'That's a relief. Could you find my friends, sir, and tell them where I am?'

'I could. Will anyone be searching for

you? And if so, how am I to know them?'

'I think Wolf will search, since he's the boss,' Charlotte said with warming cheeks. 'He's tall and dark and he rides a magnificent black stallion—you'll recognise Stormbird all right, there aren't many horses like him out here.' She remembered something, and chuckled. 'It was Stormbird that Chapaupau was after, only he reckoned without Wolf.'

M Robinaux smiled.

'And without you, from what I've heard. Your courage will be the talk of the leather lodges for a long time to come.'

'I'm beginning to think I should have behaved like an English miss and screamed and fainted,' Charlotte said ruefully. 'Then I don't suppose Chapaupau would be so keen to add me to his wives. I think he sees visions of little papooses all hurling themselves into battle, as I did.'

The Frenchman smiled.

'You're probably right. I'll search for your trail companions and perhaps we'll meet again, if I'm asked to return for the ransom.'

'Thank you, monsieur,' Charlotte said fervently. 'And good luck!'

'The same to you. Stay with the women if you possibly can and you'll be safe for a while.'

After he had gone Charlotte spoke a little more French with Ahabi, but she soon realized that the older woman's French was of the most basic sort, and availed them little. Still, it was better than nothing, and at least it saved a lot of arm-waving and face-pulling.

For the rest of that day she took M Robinaux's advice and stuck closely to the squaws. She went with Singueapech down to the river and helped her to lift two fish traps. Both traps contained fish and the squaw was pleased with her catch, killing the fish by striking their heads against the river rocks and then putting them into a reed bag which reeked of many such catches. Since it was a fine day, this was not an unpleasant task, but Charlotte guessed that it could be quite dangerous when the river was running fast and full, since they had been forced to wade almost to midstream to fetch the traps, and when they had re-baited them the whole procedure had to be done again in reverse.

The day wore on. Twice in the course

of it Chapaupau came to the entrance of the wigwam and peered in at them. Once, indeed, he came right in and sat by the fire whilst a meal was being prepared. Charlotte watched him carefully and saw that he was watching her, but apart from addressing her twice and ordering Ahabi to translate for him he did nothing. Indeed, most of his attention seemed to be absorbed by one of his sons, a fatly smiling child of two or three, who toddled over to his father and cast himself on to Chapaupau's lap with every sign of affection and trust.

'He say you brave woman,' Ahabi told her the first time the brave made her translate to Charlotte. And then, just before he left the wigwam, 'He say you beautiful, too.'

After this, fear visited Charlotte with an inspiration.

'Ahabi, teach me to say, "I belong to Wolf-Hunter, he my man," in your language,' she said. There was a short pause whilst Ahabi puzzled this out, and then, nodding energetically, she translated the remark from French into her own tongue.

Charlotte repeated the guttural sounds until she was word perfect and then, the day dusking at last, she lay down with the other women, after they had eaten some pemmican, which was rather nice, and some roast dog, which wasn't half as bad as she had anticipated, and slept once more.

It was not until she woke in the middle of the night, hot and uneasy amongst so many strange bodies, that something rather odd occurred to her. She had, voluntarily, and more than once, claimed to be 'Wolf's woman'. It would have been as simple and a good deal more accurate to have claimed to be 'Freddy's woman'. She supposed it was because if anyone rescued her Wolf was a good deal likelier to do it than Freddy, but she wondered what Wolf would think if he could have heard her claims.

Soon enough, however, she settled down to sleep again. It was her second night in the village.

Ahabi awoke her next morning and they ate coarse bread and hard boiled eggs with curiously mottled shells which Charlotte did not recognize. Afterwards, Ahabi, Singueapech and Charlotte fetched a supply of whitish roots from a storage

137

hut made from willow branches. One of the women cut these roots into manageable lengths and then the three of them pounded them until they resembled coarse flour or perhaps semolina.

Close by them, Tollamea combined two jobs—she looked after the children whilst making a fish trap, weaving the thin willow branches in and out of each other with such speed and dexterity that Charlotte could only marvel at her.

Two or three times in the course of the morning Chapaupau came over to them, made some remark to one or other of his wives and then wandered off again, but around noon, to Charlotte's great relief, he joined a party of some other braves of around his own age and they mounted their ponies and rode off across the prairie. A hunting expedition, no doubt. Charlotte pointed at them and raised her eyebrows at Ahabi, who replied in French, 'They get meat,' which seemed to indicate either a hunting trip or a raid on a neighbouring village. Since they were unpainted, Charlotte assumed it was merely a hunt.

Although Chapaupau's wives were friendly and seemed to accept her presence,

Charlotte soon noticed that such was not the case with the other women. A little girl, toddling over to her with a ball made out of animal skin, held it up to her but when Charlotte bent to take it she received a hard push and the child was snatched away, as was the ball.

'What was that in aid of?' Charlotte said crossly. 'Does she think Europeans eat babies?'

Ahabi did not understand the words, but the sense was clear enough. She thought for a moment, then spoke.

'Women say ransom best. Women's own place best,' she said at last.

'I wish Chapaupau thought the same,' Charlotte said heavily. She practised her sentence again. 'I belong Wolf-Hunter, he my man.'

Ahabi looked a little sceptical, but then they both turned back to their work.

It was dusk before the hunting party returned, and then there was rejoicing for they brought with them a huge buffalo, towing it across the prairie with rope round its mighty shoulders.

'We eat meat tonight,' Ahabi told Charlotte gleefully. 'Charlotte have hide.'

139

Charlotte eyed the bloodied and uncured skin with revulsion but tried to hide her feelings. She knew that it would rapidly begin to reek and attract flies and she had no idea how to cure it, nor whether accepting it would compromise her in some way. Fortunately, however, nothing more was required of her at that stage than the acceptance, and when they gathered round the fire Chapaupau did nothing more sinister than to see that she got her fair share of the roast meat, with two fat ears of maize as well which she very much enjoyed.

After feasting and a telling of tales which Charlotte could only guess at from the pantomime of a young brave who cavorted in the open, firelit space, some of the women got up and danced. A suggestion was made that Charlotte too should display her virtuosity in this sphere, but to her relief it was speedily vetoed by an elderly crone with a nutcracker face and a harsh, dictatorial voice. Good enough, Charlotte thought, thankfully; the waltz would not go well here, I feel sure!

As it grew darker, however, the feeling that she would not be here much longer intensified. Help, she was sure, could not be far away. So when the women left the fire and went into the big wigwam she did not attempt to lie down but combed out her hair with the bone comb that seemed to be the common property of Chapaupau's wives, brushed as many dog and buffalo hairs off her clothing as she could, and sat down, erect and ready for whatever might occur, near the entrance.

Her intuition, if such it had been, was not wrong. Not long after she had taken up her post there was a stirring amongst the braves who were still gathered in the middle of the clearing, talking, boasting, and drinking. They turned, a bit like puppets all attached to the same string, and following the direction of their eyes Charlotte saw a tall man on a tall horse ride into camp.

Pleasure and excitement rippled through her. Wolf had come, he was here, and very soon she would be on her way back to the Cuban party! She moved quickly, dodging out of the wigwam before she could be called back by the squaws and made her way in the flickering firelight towards Wolf, eager to turn the dream into reality.

He saw her, and gestured her to go back, into the wigwam. She hesitated, swallowing tears of disappointment, and then crept back into the leather lodge, though she sat down once again in the entrance. From here she could at least watch what was happening. Even Wolf would not deny her that!

But she had reckoned without the Indian love of bargaining, for the talking, boasting, promising and threatening went on all night and after three hours of it Charlotte confessed herself beaten. She just had to get some sleep! So she crawled back to the women, collapsed on to a pile of hides, and immediately forgot her troubles in slumber.

'You go now, Char-lotte. Charlotte go with Wolf-hunter.'

Ahabi was shaking her, hissing in her ear. Charlotte sat up, blinked, then shook off the furs and got to her feet. Whilst she slept, it seemed, all the arrangements had been made and she was to go right now, without further delay or parleying.

'Wolf-hunter much like,' Ahabi said enviously as she watched Charlotte tug the comb through her hair. 'Pay much ransom. Two good horses and cow with calf.'

Charlotte's eyes widened. She knew how

much store Wolf set by that calf, how pleased he was that he had brought a young bull because now he would have two cows to breed with when they reached California.

'The calf too? Oh, but surely...'

'Chapaupau make good bargain,' Ahabi said. 'Cow and calf, my man say. Just cow, no calf, your man say. Then your man want you more than he want calf.' She beamed. 'Is good, eh?'

'Is very good,' Charlotte said decidedly. After all, she could buy Wolf a couple more cows when they reached California, couldn't she? Freddy had a generous monthly allowance; he would willingly hand over the money when she explained the circumstances, she was sure.

In the clearing, rather to her surprise, Chapaupau was also mounted and apparently ready to ride, with two other braves as well. She stopped, gazing up at Wolf enquiringly.

'What's all this? Are they going to accompany us?'

Wolf scowled down at her, not at all like a man who had willingly paid a large ransom just for the pleasure of her company.

'You didn't think I'd come galloping across the prairie with a milch cow and calf under my arm, did you? To say nothing of two mules? They're coming halfway with us, to where we'll meet Mr Robinaux with the ransom beasts.'

'Oh, I see,' Charlotte said rather blankly. 'Does Chapaupau have to come, though? I don't feel terribly safe with him around.'

'Of course he must come—he's going to assert his rights pretty promptly, honey, if I don't come up with the ransom! You'd better start praying that M Robinaux manages to convince Leo of the wisdom of complying with his wishes and brings the stock.'

Charlotte swallowed. Even now it seemed she was not safe but dependent on Leo's seeing sense!

'I do pray. I'm sorry for the trouble I've caused you, but...'

As she spoke she went alongside Storm-bird until she was standing close to Wolf's knee and this caused Chapaupau to bring his pony alongside and catch her arm. Charlotte stood quite still, her eyes fixed appealingly on Wolf's face, but though she did catch a glimmer of sympathy in his eyes he shook his head.

144

'No, my child, I cannot take you up before me; you must ride with Chapaupau.'

It was unbelievable, but it was true. She rode for several hours perched uncomfortably before Chapaupau, with his arm firm about her waist. It was hateful, but she could see the sense of it. If the milch cow and calf and the two mules were not at the meeting place then she would be his, and he was not going to risk treachery.

It seemed a terribly long time to Charlotte before, in the distance, she saw a small group of animals and a couple of men. They were in the shade of a huge pillar of rock and as they rode nearer she saw that it was indeed M Robinaux, riding a roan gelding and leading two mules whilst another man, an Indian, rode a beautiful cream-coloured pony and led the milch cow and the calf.

Wolf turned in his saddle and grinned at her.

'See 'em? Your salvation, honey! Let's get this over with.'

In fact, the exchange was quick and to the point. M Robinaux waved a greeting and then spurred his horse over to Chapaupau who examined the mules, then rode over to the cow and calf and subjected them to an equally keen scrutiny before loosing his grip on Charlotte's waist. She landed neatly and hurried over to Stormbird and Wolf.

'I'll go back to the encampment with 'em, help with the stock,' M Robinaux called out. 'Girl all right?'

Charlotte, with one foot in the stirrup and both hands clasping Wolf's, felt fine, even if she did ache all over. She smiled blissfully up at Wolf and said as much. Wolf raised his voice to call to Robinaux.

'Yup, she's all right. Many thanks.'

With that, he settled her before him and turned Stormbird's head back towards the broad prairie. As the stallion lengthened his stride to an easy trot Wolf spoke.

'Well? How does it feel to be more of a nuisance than twenty-four men and twenty mules?'

Charlotte sighed. It had been so wonderful just to be free, to know that she was on her way back to the trail! But Wolf had spoiled it, as he spoiled so many things.

'I only did it to save you from getting shot! I don't expect gratitude, but...'

'Gratitude!' He was so furious that he

urged Stormbird into a canter, then had to drag the horse to a halt the better to answer her. He looked down into her face, his eyes iced water, his lips tight with temper.

'Gratitude! If you'd been where you should have been, down in the encampment getting the meal, none of this would have happened!'

'I would have been getting the meal, if you hadn't hit me! And anyway, if I hadn't shouted and attacked Chapaupau you'd have been dead! If I had been cooking, come to think of it, you'd have followed Stormbird anyway, and you'd have been shot just the same, so you'd still be dead!'

'Shot? Why should he shoot me, you silly little...'

'Because he was luring Stormbird near enough to steal, and you followed the horse,' Charlotte said, her voice rising. 'That was why I jumped him, because he'd got his rifle and was pointing it straight at you, because I knew it wouldn't be any good warning you...'

'Absolute rubbish! He might have put a bullet through my hair to scare me off but he wouldn't have killed me. He was alone, dammit, he was horse-stealing. It wouldn't have helped him to kill a white man, especially if he meant to steal Stormbird, who's pretty identifiable.'

'But he *was* going to...'

'Don't lie to me!' He was really shouting now, a dull red flash on his cheekbones, his nostrils flared with temper. 'You ran away, panicked because you saw an Indian near, and got taken. Lucky for you I thought it worthwhile to follow and lucky for you I brought you back, because if I hadn't you'd have been his for good, with a half-breed papoose in nine months, very like.'

'I would not!' Her temper sizzling, Charlotte was shouting every bit as loudly as he. 'I'd sooner kill myself than submit to a man like that!'

Abruptly, it seemed, the violence which had been so near the surface left him. He looked down into her red and furious face and laughed. It seemed to Charlotte a sinister sound.

'You've spent two nights in an Indian village as a prospective bride to one of the braves. I've bought you back with my own stock. So though you may not be Chapaupau's, you're mine, fair and square! The only difference is I'll marry you decently, to save your folk from shame.'

She was so astonished that for a moment she could only stare, round-eyed, but she soon found her tongue.

'Wha-at? Marry me? Me, marry you? I'm not going to marry anyone, or not until I get to California, at any rate.'

He clicked his tongue and Stormbird began to move forward once more. His arm tightened about her waist, reminding her wordlessly of his physical strength and equally of his physical magnetism. She might talk very big, but she would not be able to resist his lovemaking once he started, and she suspected that they both knew it. But the knowledge gave her a new and desperate strength—she could not marry him, she had seen too much of men who liked Indians, liked the country, and took themselves a string of squaws to wife. Oh, he might be too proud to marry Indian women, but he was not too proud to lie with them! And anyway, there was Freddy. He needed her to keep house for him, to keep him out of mischief, too. Marriage was out of the question.

'You'll do as you're told. You can marry me or be my woman—take your choice. If you prefer marriage, I'm agreeable. If not,

I'll move back into my tent and take you anyway.'

He spoke quite calmly, but Charlotte felt fear and excitement course through her. He meant it, she had no doubt of that. She considered the situation as well as she could. She was helpless, of course, if he chose to take her. But on the other hand, surely if she married him such a marriage, conducted under duress, could not be legally binding? She could get it annulled once they reached California and go to Freddy just as she had planned. She began to feel a bit better. She would agree to it, and anyway, they might not be able to find anyone to marry them in this wilderness.

'I'd sooner marry than be your mistress.' She said it sulkily, but he ignored her tone and briefly caressed her cheek with his fingers. She felt her heart begin to beat more quickly and cursed her own stupid susceptibility to his touch.

'Good. Then we'll have a truce till we reach the Slough. Waggon trains tend to pile up there as the parties prepare for the crossing. We're bound to find a preacher there.'

They remained silent for several miles

and then Charlotte said tentatively: 'Look, you don't want to marry me and I don't want to be married, so why can't I just pay you back for the cows and things? We needn't tell anyone that I was with the Indians all the time.'

'Keep that a secret? With twenty-four men telling everyone we meet that they've lost the woman who's been travelling with them? With the French fur trapper and his wife seeing you being handed over like a parcel? You *are* an optimist!'

'His wife? Where was she?' Charlotte said, momentarily diverted. 'I only saw a young Indian brave.'

'No, she's a squaw; pretty little thing. He dresses her in men's clothing when he takes her near white folk; says there isn't much honour amongst us concerning Indian women, which I'm bound to say is fair comment.'

'Yes,' Charlotte said ominously. 'You like squaws and you don't like me much, so why should you suffer?'

He turned and looked down at her, his eyes travelling over her in a way which they never had before, until a blush burned from the top of her head to the tip of her toes.

'I don't think I'll suffer too much,' he said pensively. 'Reckon I'll bear the pain of having an uppity, sassy woman in my bed without too much complaint.'

Charlotte bit back a giggle and fixed her eyes sternly in front of her.

'That wasn't exactly what I meant. But there's no point in trying to argue with you in this mood.'

'No point at all,' he agreed peaceably, and the great horse thundered on.

CHAPTER 6

They rejoined the Cuban party as night was falling, and received a tumultuous welcome, but eager though they were to hear about the rescue the men could hardly wait to describe their own tribulations.

'We lost Abbersley,' Leo said as soon as the wanderers sat down and addressed themselves to roast sage hen and lambs greens with a side helping of friend onions. 'Yessir, not a thing we could do to save him. Shot hisself in the belly.'

'That's dreadful,' Charlotte said. 'How

on earth did he come to do a thing like that?'

Leo shrugged, mouth full of chicken.

'Accident, I guess. A dirty gun-barrel, perhaps. Any road, he's dead.'

'What else?' Wolf said resignedly, taking a draught of brandy and water. 'No more deaths?'

'Jeez, no, ain't one enough? But we've been travelling nights, 'cos the days was too hot. And Matthew's mule's gone. Took by a freshwater shark I reckon, though Matthew says it trod in a pothole. There one minute, gone the next! More hen?'

'Just disappeared?' Charlotte said. 'A freshwater shark...what are you talking about, Leo?'

The men gathered round gave a shout of laughter and Leo explained that the mule had disappeared whilst crossing a deep, fast-running river.

'Oh I *see*,' Charlotte said, relieved that there was a rational explanation. 'What else?'

'That's enough, ain't it? 'Cep that durn devil-goat of yourn ate her way through a sack o' corn and kicked the bucket over three times whilst I was milkin' her.'

'That's nothing new,' Charlotte admitted. 'And don't call her my goat, she's Wolf's, he bought her.'

'That reminds me,' Wolf drawled. 'I'm marryin' Charlotte. Anyone seen a preacher?'

In the short silence that followed Charlotte thought how typical of the man the announcement was. Not 'I've asked Charlotte to marry me', or 'Charlotte and I are getting married', but 'I'm marrying Charlotte'. A statement of intent. Typical, she thought bitterly. Absolutely typical!

It appeared that a preacher had been seen by virtually every man present, and everyone was keen to tell Wolf where the man might be found, so there was little point in Charlotte hoping for a reprieve. Marriage it was to be!

'Good. Then he can tie the knot before we cross the desert,' Wolf said briskly, getting to his feet. 'I'll arrange it for tomorrow.'

That night Charlotte had several nightmares, mostly concerning preachers and all concerning marriage. When she woke, she lay for a moment looking at the sun shining on the canvas of her tent and telling herself that it would never happen.

154

It couldn't, because no preacher would marry her to Wolf when he heard all she had to say on the subject and realized she was being coerced.

So it was strange that when the Reverend Packer came to see her, talking gently and kindly about marriage and its various responsibilities, she never said one word to disillusion him about her willingness. She smiled, and took her place by Wolf's side, and tried not to blush when the service was read, especially when it came to repeating the sentences concerned with worshipping bodies—it was enough to make a squaw blush, thought Charlotte, scarlet-cheeked. It saddened her that not once did Wolf look at her, except when the preacher told him to produce the ring. Then he took her hand and his eyes, dark with some emotion unfathomable to her, met hers.

He's not thought of the ring, Charlotte told herself, halfway between glee and a sick disappointment, but she wronged him; he had thought of everything. He separated her fingers, then slid on to her engagement finger an absolutely plain, slim gold band. It was a little large, but not enough to matter. She looked up into his face, wide-eyed, to see him still looking

155

down at her, his eyes slumbrous, heavy, even as his fingers gripped hers tightly for a moment before releasing them.

After that, the ceremony was almost over. The preacher congratulated them, calling her Mrs McCall, which startled her very much at first since she had always assumed that Wolf was his surname; now it appeared that it was a nickname he had managed to pick up. I wonder how, Charlotte thought sarcastically, remembering the way he could bark and snarl.

Leo had prepared a special supper, borrowing and begging from other waggons waiting in the Slough, so they fared well, and after the meal Charlotte actually accepted a mug of whisky and water which she found less hateful than she had expected it to be. After she had drunk it she found that she, too, was laughing at the jokes, many of which she did not understand, and singing the songs. At one point she saw her husband was watching her gravely and she smiled up at him coquettishly.

'Well? It's what you wanted, isn't it?'

'Wanted? Perhaps. Are you drunk, Charlotte? I've never seen you take spirits before.'

'It's Dutch courage,' Charlotte said. She spoke too loudly, she knew it, but she seemed incapable of dropping her voice. 'Never mind, tomorrow we cross the desert and then it's all downhill to California.'

Wolf laughed.

'Downhill? Once we've crossed the desert we face the Sierra Nevada Mountains-the Rockies, folk call 'em. That's the worst part of the trail, far worse than the desert because they go on for so much longer. That's where mules sicken and die from the pulling, and men begin to give up.'

'Oh, well, better look on them as the gateway to California. What'll you do when we get there, Wolf?'

He was still looking at her uneasily, as if he thought she might do something stupid at any moment. When he gets me alone he'll tell me off for drinking that whisky, she thought to herself. I must see that he doesn't get me alone!

And then it struck her that they would be alone very soon now. She felt a cold trickle of uncertainty strike even through the warmth which the spirit had engendered. She did not want to be married now, to go into that little tent and let Wolf do...whatever it was that husbands did.

She was standing close to him and she shivered, a great big shudder that shook her from head to foot. Without thinking, she clutched Wolf's sleeve.

'I feel funny,' she said.

'Uh-huh, too much to drink.'

He picked her up without ceremony and walked, with her in his arms, towards their tent. There was a cheer from the men and Charlotte hid her face against his chest.

'Carry you over the threshold,' Wolf explained, except that it was not possible to enter their tiny tent save on one's knees so he had to kneel, bundle her inside, and then crawl in after her. She crossed the tent still on her knees, then turned to face him, eyeing him uncertainly in the flickering lantern light which Leo had brought in earlier.

'I still feel funny.'

'Yup. Get undressed.'

Though it was hot during the day out here, it was very cold at nights. Charlotte hoped he would put her shivering down to the cold. She sat down on her bedroll and pulled off her doeskin tunic and her breeches, because her shirt reached her knees and was quite respectable. She looked across at Wolf, who was stripping quite unhurriedly and apparently without a care, though to her relief he stopped at his breeches. Their bedrolls were together but he came over, pulled them a little apart, and then lay down on his. She continued to sit on her own bedroll, her legs tucked under her, brushing her hair. Wolf smiled at her, one of his nicest smiles. Charlotte's heart began to patter.

'Get into bed or you'll freeze. Right now!'

She obeyed in scrambling haste. Did this mean that tonight would not be devoted to embarrassing, if biblical, behaviour?

When he saw that she was covered and comfortable, he leaned up on one elbow and turned out the lantern. Then he lay down again. Charlotte, illogically, felt rather disappointed. Was he not even going to kiss her goodnight? She peered at him through the thick darkness, and could just about make out his face.

'Goodnight, Wolf.'

'Night, Charlotte.'

'It's awfully cold, isn't it! Shall we move our bedrolls together?'

The moment the words were out she felt dreadful. Whatever had made her say that? How brazen he would think her! It must be the whisky. She would never drink the wretched stuff again.

She saw his teeth gleam in a brief, hard smile, but when he answered her, it was indulgently. He still thought her drunk, thank goodness!

'Not tonight, Charlotte. We've got the desert crossing tomorrow and after that the Sierra Nevada. We'll talk about it again in California.'

For a moment she lay in the dark, feeling bereft, cheated. Then, as his words sank in, her heart lifted a little. Did he mean that though he had married her, he would not take her as his wife until they reached California? If that was so, it was best of all, for the moment they touched California soil she intended to run away from him!

The men had been told the previous day that they would not start to cross the Humboldt desert until late afternoon, so they spent a luxurious morning sleeping, got up at noon for a combined breakfast and lunch and finally set off, with all the beasts well fed and watered for what would be a long and parching crossing, as the sun was sinking in the west.

It was evening when they reached the Humboldt Sink itself. Charlotte, who had grown used to hard country, thought that this was the strangest and hardest of the lot. The ground was burning white so dazzling that it hurt the eyes to look upon on it and strewn over the chalky wastes were more dead beasts than they had seen so far. In the centre of this burning valley was the sink itself where the Humboldt finally vanished, a stinking morass of reeds and long, rank grass. As they passed, mirages formed and shimmered around them, causing the men to blink and rub their eyes, doubting their own senses.

The smell was very bad but Charlotte, sitting easily on Tandy, set her lips and endured. When Wolf rode by, however, she called out to him.

'Wolf, wouldn't it be quicker if we didn't overnight here? I've heard folk say that it's better to simply keep going until you reach the other side.'

Wolf, his hat brim tilted to shade his eyes though the sun was long gone, shook his head.

'That's the way folk lost all their stock—no, we'll continue as we planned and we'll have fewer losses. We've brought all the water we can carry and enough grass for four days.'

'But surely...'

A smouldering glance, shot at her from beneath his hat-brim, caused Charlotte's voice to fade away. There was little point in the argument, after all, since Wolf had made his mind up, and in truth she had only started the questions so that he would stay with her for a little while. Leo was ahead and she was bored, here in the rear by herself.

But when Wolf came to the spot he had chosen to camp, she did rebel. It was close by some sulphur springs which, though they smelt awful, were said to be harmless to beasts and man, which was why Wolf had chosen the spot, of course. It would conserve their fresh water for another few hours. But behind the springs was a treacherous bog where a great many cattle and mules had become mired up to their necks and been abandoned by their previous owners, dying slowly and with many a vain bellow or neigh for help when they heard the Cuban party nearby. Wolf told Charlotte that it was useless for her to grieve for they could not help the animals; they must just do their best to see that their own beasts did not suffer a similar fate. But even he looked a little less than satisfied at the continual noise, and the fearful smell from the gasses of animals long dead and half sunk in the mire ensured that little sleep could be had by any member of the party.

Charlotte went to her tent in high dudgeon, lay down, and let black thoughts crowd her mind. When Wolf followed her he seemed to know that she was awake for he held out a hand and took hers where it lay outside her coverings.

'Charlotte? Try to sleep.'

'How can I?' She tried to speak calmly, but her bitterness could not be disguised. 'Those poor creatures. It's heartless to sleep when they're in such agony. Couldn't we shoot them so at least they die quickly?'

'You know we can't spare the ammunition. There's nothing any of us can do!' He sounded impatient, short tempered, and very weary. 'Get some rest and you'll be fitter to continue the rest of the journey.'

Charlotte snuggled down, muttering beneath her breath, but he heard.

'What was that? Speak louder if you've anything worth saying.'

'I said we should have kept going, like I wanted to.'

He said nothing more, perhaps because he felt she was right, but after four of the longest hours of wakeful misery that Charlotte had ever lived through she heard him stir, and then get up and leave the tent. Eagerly, she leaned up on her elbow. What was he going to do? He had insisted that all their stock be tethered so that they couldn't wander, so there was no hope of setting forth in the middle of the night. It would take them hours and hours to untie all the animals in the dark.

She waited, but he did not come back. The obvious reason, that he had gone to answer a call of nature, could no longer apply; he had been gone far too long. She could not hear anyone talking, but the bellowing of one of the wide-horned oxen in the swamp would drown all but the loudest conversation. She climbed out of her blankets, pulled on her breeches and boots and slung her cloak round her, for it was very cold. She would have to go and make sure that he had not ended up caught in the bog himself.

She went out, into the bright moonlight. It gave the scene a truly hell-like clarity, with the dying beasts, the dead and the living all silver and black, whilst the stink of putrefaction ensured that the living could not rest. From where she stood she could see Tandy, pricking up her ears and shifting from foot to foot. She looked past the mule, and nearly died of shock. She had been right to come out. Wolf was up to his knees in the bog! She rushed forward, her heart beating a tattoo of terror in her breast. What on earth had happened? Had he been sleepwalking, wandered into the mire? Would he go further yet?

She reached the edge of the bog and Wolf turned and saw her. He looked rather annoyed.

'Keep back, Charlotte,' he said crisply. 'You can stand there and take hold of her when I drag her clear, if you want to help.'

Charlotte looked further, and of course it was that evil-smelling, devil-reared goat who had chewed through her tether and gone marching straight into the bog, her udder pulling her hindquarters down further and quicker than her forequarters, so that she looked as if she were almost beyond hope. Damn her eyes, Charlotte thought with a savagery which amazed her. If Wolf dies trying to rescue that stupid, vicious goat...

She went right up to the quaking edge of the bog, ignoring his instructions to keep back. He took another step forward, testing the depth, and this time he sank deeper. Charlotte stepped on to a tuft of thick, sulphurous grass herself, felt it wobble, but held her ground.

'Come back, Wolf, she's not worth it! *Please*, Wolf, you're the trail boss, we can't manage without you.'

'She's our milk supply now that the other cow's in calf. We can't manage without her, either. Have you seen Sally?'

'She's safe,' Charlotte said wildly. She had not, in fact, the remotest idea where the kid was. 'Please, Wolf, I beg you to come back.'

'Not till I get her out.'

Another six feet of bog separated him from the goat and even as they watched Emily gave her stupid, breathless ba-aa and managed, somehow, to lurch forward deeper into the mire. Wolf used a word Charlotte had never heard before, tugged one booted foot almost free and plunged it in again, further out. And deeper. He was a lot heavier than the goat, of course, and would sink much sooner. Charlotte sighed, shivered a little, and then splashed right into the bog. Wolf turned at the sound, his black brows drawing together in a frown of ominous proportions.

'Get out of here, you silly little bitch. Do as you're told or I'll beat hell out of you when I get back to shore!'

'No! Get out yourself! You told me I was to look after Emily, it was my job to remember that she eats rope when she feels like it. Wolf, would you please stop being pigheaded and *think?* Why do you suppose Emily has got so far without sinking, when she's passed dead mules and dead oxen? It's because she's lighter than they are. If you'll come out right now, on to dry land, then I'll go forward, grab that hateful goat by the collar, and bring her nearer so that you can lift her out. I can do it because I'm ever so much lighter than you are. Please?' She saw him hesitate as the truth of her words sank in. 'Please, Wolf! I swear if I think it's too dangerous I'll come right out, I swear it! Please?'

'It makes sense.' He said it grudgingly and, as he said it, turned back to the shore. 'But you'll come back the minute

I say? You swear it?'

She nodded eagerly. She would have agreed to anything to get him out of that bog.

'I swear. Come on!'

It took him longer than he had expected to get back on to solid ground once more and a good deal more effort, too. His chest was heaving by the time he stood on the shore again and sweat stood out on his brow, but she did not reproach him for the risk he had taken. She stepped out herself, feeling the awful suck and surge of the bog, the way the whole place rocked when one of the trapped animals made a last, desperate move.

It was a nightmare to keep on moving forward, going deeper and deeper. But after what seemed like hours of inching onward, she stretched out her hand and caught hold of Emily, not by her collar to be sure, but by her horrid little tufted tail. She gave a shriek of triumph.

'I've got her! Wolf, I've got her! Can you throw me a rope?'

For the first time she half turned towards the encampment, and got the shock of her life. Every man was out of his bed and standing poised at the edge of the bog and every man was cheering, shouting, even jumping up and down until Wolf hushed them and began to speak, with a tiny shake in his voice that she was at a loss to understand.

'Charlotte, listen to me! I'm going to throw the rope with a billet of wood tied to it so's it reaches you and falls near. Tie it round Emily's stomach—can you do that? Don't try to reach her collar, just get it round her stomach. Then keep a hand on the rope and I'll haul you both in.'

The first throw was perfect, the billet of wood landed right on Emily's bony backside with a satisfying clonk. The goat had finally realized that she was in trouble and far from trying to go further forward she actually seemed to be trying to turn in Charlotte's direction. However, even with Emily's co-operation, Charlotte found it impossible to circumnavigate the goat's belly with the rope. Whenever she tried she either got tangled up in Emily's back legs or found herself foiled by the full udder. In the end, with a sigh, she tried the rope round her own waist, held on to Emily's tail with both hands, and asked Wolf, in a voice which cracked with exhaustion, to pull like hell.

One pull was enough to heave her knees free from the clinging mud and to get most of Emily's hindquarters out in the open. It also almost fulfilled Charlotte's ambition to possess a sixteen-inch waist, though at the time she merely screamed at Wolf that he was tearing her in two, and fortunately he realized that she had other plans and slackened his hold on the rope so that she could untie it from her own waist and put it round Emily's, whilst still holding the animal's tail up in the air at a very undignified angle. It was not easy, for the mud-laden goat was heavy and Charlotte's arms were tired, but she managed it at last, just as dawn began to break in the east.

It took thirty more minutes of back-breaking work to bring the goat and herself out on to the bank and collapse, covered in mud, blood and rope burns. But triumphant. She just managed to say 'I *told* you...' before Wolf picked her up in his arms, carried her over to the nearest sulphur spring, and dumped her unceremoniously in it.

'Strip off,' he said briefly. 'I'll wash out your shirt and breeches whilst you wash yourself.'

'I couldn't possibly,' Charlotte said

weakly, clinging to his hands whilst the soft, queer-smelling water eased some of the aches from her body. 'I'll wash with my clothes on.'

Wolf glanced behind him, to where the men were gathering round the chuck waggon. Leo was lighting a fire, preparing a meal of some sort. He sighed.

'You're right, for the second time in one night. Your head will be so swollen you'll be unbearable tomorrow!' He helped her out of the water and put an arm round her. 'Here, let's get you back to the tent, then you can strip in private and I'll see your things are clean and dry by tomorrow.'

'It is tomorrow,' Charlotte pointed out, glowing with his nearness, basking in the warmth of his approval. 'We'll be leaving here soon, won't we? Well, I'll dry myself and put my spare clothes on and come out and help get the meal.'

'You'll do nothing of the sort. You're going to ride in the waggon. Don't argue. I'll wrap you in both bedrolls and give you some whisky and perhaps that way you won't suffer from chills or fever or whatever it is people get from mud baths.'

'Mud baths are good for you,' Charlotte said sleepily, as they entered the tent.

'People in England have mud baths for their complexions, I believe. I've probably had enough free beauty treatment to last me a year!'

'You don't need it.' The words were spoken quietly, almost absently, but the look which accompanied them said a lot more. 'When you're dry just wrap the blankets round you and I'll come back and carry you over to the waggon. You'll sleep, see if you don't.'

She did, once she had got over her starry-eyed wonder at his words. He had as good as told her she was beautiful! From such a taciturn and forthright man as Wolf, that was a compliment to treasure. And, just for a moment, he had sounded...quite fond of her. She wrapped the blankets round herself and settled down to dream a little.

Charlotte slept the clock round after her ordeal, to wake, positively bouncing with vitality, when the camp began to stir on the third day of their journey. She popped her head out of the unlaced waggon opening and shouted. A dozen heads turned in her direction and a dozen mouths smiled widely. Charlotte smiled back.

'Is this breakfast? Can I have some? I'm starving. I wish you'd woken me sooner!'

There was a gust of laughter and Wolf appeared and came over to the waggon, trying unsuccessfully not to smile.

'Hi there! You're awake, I see, but not starving, surely? I fed you porridge and soup and all sorts yesterday and you ate the lot without even opening your eyes.'

'I did?' Charlotte said wonderingly. 'Well, I'm starving now, so save me some porridge!'

'We will. It's made with Emily's milk; that's a remarkable goat. She milked fresh and pure within a couple of hours of being dragged ass first out of that durned mire.'

'That's good,' Charlotte said vaguely. 'I won't be long.'

She disappeared into the waggon again and emerged ten minutes later, spruce and fresh in a clean shirt and breeches. There was a good deal of bustle as the men prepared to move off, but she was glad to see that Leo had saved her a large dish of porridge and a mug of coffee.

'Just you git outside of these,' he said, handing her the plate and mug. 'We're camping at Hot Springs tonight. You wouldn't want to miss *them;* first real water since we hit the desert—and weird, too.'

'Hot Springs? How hot? And how do you know about them?'

Leo, watching her spoon porridge, smiled indulgently.

'Every traveller knows about the Hot Springs, Charlotte! Sides, Mr Hobbs told tales about 'em, last night. Says you can boil an egg straight off, and mek coffee without a fire!'

'Huh!' said Charlotte, finishing her porridge, draining her coffee, and standing the empty mug and dish down beside her. 'A likely story. You'd think old Hobbs would be more careful, knowing we're going to visit the place.'

'Wait 'n see,' Leo said. 'Gee, Charlotte, you sure are a heroine! We'll boast about you when we git to where the waggons meet up agin by the Truckee River. 'Twaren't only th' old goat you saved. Wolf reckoned it might've gone bad for him if you hadn't happened along.'

Charlotte could not help a gratified smile appearing on her face.

'Wolf said that? Gracious! And he pretended he was right as rain, up to his thighs in mud.'

174

'Aw, that's just his way. Reckon he felt purty bad when you were out there an' all—never seen a man sweat like it.'

'Is that so?' If fear and love could be measured in buckets of sweat, she must have shed a good few pailfuls herself when she had walked out of the tent and seen him so perilously placed. In that moment she had seen that he was a good man, a man who deserved better than to die to save a stupid goat. A man moreover, whom she would have been happy to be married to, if only circumstances had been different and he less easily attracted to any woman who happened to be around. Sometimes, she wondered if he *did* like her a little, for all his harshness, but if he had he would not have just turned away from her on their wedding night.

Sometimes she surprised a look in his eye, quickly banished, which made her hopeful that one day he might see that she was a good deal more to his taste than Indian squaws. But at other times, especially when they were at odds, she felt that the sooner he took off with a squaw and left her alone the better.

Men, she decided sagely, going into the waggon to pack her things, took a deal

175

of understanding, and she simply did not have the time at the moment to try to fathom this particular specimen out.

They reached Hot Springs by late afternoon and settled down fairly near the big central pool. There were a number of springs round the pool which was perhaps thirty yards in circumference, and very warm. Some of the springs were boiling, some were merely lukewarm and others sent jets of steam hissing into the air. Mr Hobbs had told no more than the truth and everyone marvelled, though they were rather cast down by the amount of property which had been abandoned here. It showed them that not everyone had been as fortunate as they in passing through this terrible country. Waggons had been abandoned, mining equipment simply left to rot, and even machinery worth a great deal of money had been regretfully cast aside since the owners knew they would never get further whilst carrying it.

The Cuban party, however, were looking well, all things considered. The mules, though weary, were still pulling, the cattle were keeping up, and the men were looking forward to a real drink and a real rest, when they had crossed the sand the next day.

'Is there any cooled water?' Wolf called out as soon as they had all assembled round the big pool. 'If so, it should go to the mules first. They've had a long haul.'

All around the pool there were casks and kegs which each train would fill before they left so that the following train would have cold water.

'Are you sure it's all right to drink?' Charlotte said suspiciously, bending over a cask of cool but evil-smelling water. 'We don't want anyone being ill, do we?'

'It's all right,' Wolf said shortly. 'Others have drunk it.'

Accordingly the mules were watered, and the horses, then the cattle and finally the men themselves, though due to its odd taste no one was very keen. Wolf, to show them all that it was harmless, boiled a quantity and made a large pot of coffee and then drank it all since no one else wanted much.

That night, after they had eaten and had a measure of whisky each, they sat by the fire for a while, talking. Wolf was first to make a move, standing up and reminding them brusquely that the next day was the one they would all find the hardest. It meant a trek of about ten miles across deep, soft sand, very hard on the mules and the waggons they pulled, as well as on the horses.

'Everyone who rides horseback will set out at dawn and go right across to the other side,' he told them. 'There they'll water their mounts and themselves, and then return with full water casks to meet the waggoners and their animals.'

Soon after that they all went off to bed and Charlotte cuddled down beneath her blankets and wondered whether to tell Wolf how worried she had been when she saw him in the swamp. But it soon became apparent that Wolf was not in the best of tempers. He answered all her attempts to talk with grunts and in the end Charlotte became offended and turned her back on him, determined to fall asleep if only to annoy him!

She woke when he did, because he leaned over and shook her, none too gently.

'Charlotte, get up. It's time we left.'

It felt like the middle of the night still, but when they crept out of the tent and Charlotte began to light the fire, which was made of pieces of an abandoned waggon, and to cook the breakfast porridge, she could see the faint line of light on the eastern horizon which heralded the dawn.

Only six of them were riding ahead—Charlotte, Leo, Wolf, and three other men whom Charlotte knew far less well. They set off when the camp was stirring, having fed the remains of their dried grass to the mules who would pull the waggons over the sand later that day, into a morning which promised to be extremely hot.

They had not gone above two miles when Charlotte realized that Wolf was in the devil of a temper. She did not know why, she just knew that it was so. And after only another fifteen minutes' riding she saw the other men realized it too, and for the most part they fell silent or dropped back to talk amongst themselves. Charlotte tried a few harmless remarks and got her head bitten off each time, so she fell silent too, though she could and did fume at his rudeness and ingratitude. How could he behave like a bear with a sore head right at the start of the worst part of the crossing?

Once they reached the sand, however, no one worried about Wolf's temper, because they were too busy coping with their own ills. The heat was cruel, there was not so much as a blade of grass in sight, thirst plagued them all and the horses could only flatten their ears and plod incredibly slowly on through the deep, burning sand.

Leo realized that they were nearing the Truckee River first. He said, his voice a croak, 'Look!' and when they followed the direction of his pointing finger they saw, on the horizon, green trees, shimmering in the heat, and the far gleam of water.

It was not a mirage, either. An hour later they were on their knees by that same river, taking cooling draughts of the delicious water. Their mounts were quickly knee-deep in the flood, watering themselves without encouragement, and then, reluctantly, both humans and animals quit the water and faced back towards that shimmering, much-hated desert.

'Fill the casks,' Wolf ordered, and proceeded to fill his own, sling them over Stormbird's back and then remount, sitting his horse apparently impervious to the fact that Charlotte, having filled her first cask, could not budge it an inch from the river bank.

'I'll do it, Charlotte,' Leo said, seeing

180

that Wolf was ignoring his wife's predicament. 'Gee, it'll be no joke ridin' that ways with full casks abangin' agin our knees!'

Wolf turned at that, stiffly, as if his neck hurt him.

'She'll stay here.'

'No I won't,' Charlotte said at once. 'I want to go back and take the others their water. I don't want to stay here by myself.' She went and stood by Stormbird's stirrup, looking up into Wolf's face. 'Wolf? What's the matter?'

'Nothing. You stay...' He stopped speaking and she saw the pallor of his face change to a sickly green. He clutched his side, swaying in the saddle. 'Stay here,' he repeated when he could speak. Sweat funnelled down the sides of his face and into the handkerchief round his neck. He looked deathly ill.

'Wolf, dismount at once,' Charlotte ordered. 'You're ill, you can't ride out like that.'

He said nothing, seeming to be struggling to speak. Then he collapsed, sagging forward on to Stormbird's neck.

Leo hurried over, waving back the other men who would have come as well.

'I thought there was somethin' wrong

when he snarled the way he did. You stay here with him, Charlotte, whilst we tek the water back to th' others. We shan't be long.'

Charlotte turned the big stallion back towards the river and Stormbird followed as meekly as a child.

'Yes, I'll stay. You take Tandy, though, Leo, with my water casks. And Stormbird, of course.'

Leo caught hold of Tandy's bridle, but chuckled at the suggestion that he should lead the stallion.

'Stormbird won't leave Wolf. Ne'er mind, he won't let anyone hurt either of you, so you'll be safe enough until we come through again.'

Stormbird certainly showed no inclination to follow the men and their mounts as they set off back into the desert once more, but Charlotte had no way of knowing whether this was loyalty to his master or an understandable distaste for the desert crossing. However, it was certainly true that when she lowered Wolf carefully to the ground and laid him gently on the cool grass in the shelter of the cotton wood trees, Stormbird did not wander off to graze as most horses would have done, but stayed nearby, grazing from time to time, but keeping a watchful eye on Wolf nevertheless. His presence comforted Charlotte, too, for Wolf showed no signs of returning consciousness for the first twenty minutes that she was alone with him.

After that time, however, his lids flickered and he looked blankly up at her.

'Charl...you?' His voice was thick and slurred, his eyes pain-filled. She nodded, wiping his forehead with her wetted handkerchief.

'Yes, it's me. You're rather ill, so we're stopping here for a little while.'

'Umm.' His lids closed again, but presently he said: 'Pain. In the guts.'

'I wonder if it was the water?' Charlotte mused uneasily. 'If so, perhaps I ought to make you vomit. Only I don't know how, until the waggons get here.'

A faint smile flickered across his countenance though he did not open his eyes.

'Good,' he said weakly. 'Jus' leave me.'

It was nightfall before all the waggons were congregated on the banks of the Truckee, and by that time Charlotte was terribly worried about Wolf. Even the wise Mr

Hobbs could give no reason for his sudden illness, because it was well-known that one could drink the water from the Hot Springs without ill effects, though people seldom indulged as deeply as Wolf had.

'It must be that,' Charlotte said worriedly. 'He's poisoned, I know he is, and I don't know what to do to make him well again.'

'Give him salt and water,' someone suggested, but Charlotte was not prepared to risk it. She kept thinking that if the water really had been bad then he would have vomited already and he had not done so. It might be some awful stomach complaint, appendicitis, wasn't it called, which needed a doctor, medical treatment, perhaps even surgery. Certainly her amateur efforts could do no good.

Finally, she sought Leo out.

'Leo, do you remember that waggon train that arrived at the beginning of the desert just as we did, in the Slough, I mean? They intended to set out later. Wasn't there a doctor with them?'

Leo slapped his thigh.

'You're right, gal. Dr Anderson. Yessir, I remember it well. Want me to ride back, see if I can bring him over ahead of the rest?'

'I think I'd better go myself,' Charlotte said carefully. 'He might not come for you, Leo, but for a distraught wife—I could burst into tears or something.'

'I sure didn't know you felt that strongly,' Leo drawled. 'You're always actin' like you hate him.'

'Don't Leo. That was before we were married.' Charlotte felt her face begin to glow. 'Anyway, I'd get a doctor for anyone, particularly the leader of an expedition; we need him, don't we?'

Leo laughed and clapped her on the shoulder.

'Guess we do. I was only teasin', gal. But I'm coming with you; ain't nothin' else I can do for Wolf.'

And that, in the end, was what they did, for Leo was adamant that no one should ride out into that shifting, treacherous sand alone and Charlotte was happy to have his company. The two of them did not wait for any more light than that provided by the moon but set out at once, glad to face the desert in the dark rather than by the light of the cruel sun.

'So you see, doctor, if you could only come back with us...' Charlotte said pleadingly.

They had found the doctor without any trouble since his party had chosen to camp right at the edge of the sands, and they had been lucky in that Leo had recognized the medical man's waggon so that they only had to disturb one man and were not forced to apply to the trail boss, who might have thought poorly of his doctor's being spirited away just before the worst part of the crossing.

And there was no doubt that Charlotte's persuasion did the trick, though not in quite the manner she had anticipated. The doctor, a young and handsome man, was dithering, when he suddenly leaned forward and said: 'I've a lady-friend in New York—hope to bring her out here next year, if I do well.'

'That'll be nice,' Charlotte said with interest. She saw that this was leading up to something, but she did not quite know what. 'Is she fond of the open spaces?'

He grinned engagingly at her.

'Dunno. But she'd sure like a little gold necklet like the one you're wearing.'

Charlotte immediately unfastened it and held it out.

'I'd love her to have it. Tell her you were given it for saving a man's life. You *will* come, won't you?'

He nodded briskly, pocketing the necklet.

'Yes. I'll tell my tent pardner that I'll fetch back some water, that'll still any complaints. My mount's tethered, so it won't take me long to saddle up.'

He was as good as his word and dawn had not broken by the time the three of them re-entered Wolf's waggon, for he had been moved from the tiny, cramped confines of the tent to what was beginning to be known as 'the sick waggon' since anyone who could neither ride nor walk was carried in it.

'His temper's fearful,' Charlotte warned the doctor, as he bent over his sleeping patient. 'He hates being ill, of course—oh, if only it's nothing serious!'

It was not.

'There's a deal of nitre in that water, he's got nitre poisoning,' the doctor said presently, after a very thorough examination. 'He wants his system irrigating more than anything—I'll show you how to brew a herb tea which will do fine if you can get it into him, but drink it he

187

must. Has be been taking liquids?'

'No,' Charlotte admitted. 'He's terribly stubborn, doctor, and he says it starts the pain again to drink. He just clenches his teeth and turns his head away when you hold a mug to his lips.'

The doctor grinned.

'A bride won't have much trouble getting her husband to drink, I'm sure. I'll give you a list of the herbs you'll need, though I'll fetch the first lot myself and brew it up for you, then you'll be able to get more. They're simple stuff. You'll find 'em all within a hundred yards of the waggon, I guess.'

The herb tea was duly brewed and when the doctor had left, with full water casks for his party, Charlotte returned to Wolf's side with a mug of the stuff, feeling hopeful that, having slept, her husband would wake in a better frame of mind.

She had difficulty sitting him up and when she had got him more or less upright and propped up with pillows he half-opened his eyes, saw the mug, and hit out with boths hands, narrowly missing the tea. Charlotte knew that when he drank at first he would suffer from violent cramping stomach pains, but the doctor had told her that these would have to be endured and would soon wear off as the tea began to have a beneficial effect. He also warned her that there might be other painful results of the irrigation, but since he did not seem able to be more specific Charlotte decided to worry about them when they occurred and not before.

Now, she explained to Wolf that he must suffer the pains for a short period in order to get better. He was staring at her vaguely, his eyes unfocused, but he did not seem as aggressive as he had been earlier. She tilted the mug to his lips.

He took a mouthful, shouted, and spat it in the general direction of his attentive wife, then lay down and turned his face away from her.

When she tried, gently, to turn him over he hit out, landing her a hard blow in the stomach with his elbow.

Charlotte gritted her teeth, caught hold of his hair and dragged him, swearing dreadfully, into a sitting position. Then she ground the tin mug against his lips.

'Drink it, damn you,' she said fiercely. 'This is an order, Captain. It'll do you good, so drink it!'

'I'll do no...'

His protests ended in a gurgle as she ruthlessly tipped herb tea down his throat. He gagged, then doubled up, clutching his stomach.

'I'm poisoned—my belly!'

She waited until the spasm eased and then wiped the sweat off his forehead with her handkerchief.

'Well done. Now some more. The doctor says it'll soon stop being painful to drink once the herbs get to work. Come on, Wolf, just take the rest of this mugful.'

He shook his head, eyeing her with dislike, then his eyes seemed to focus on her and he leaned closer, peering at her shirt where it opened into a v at the neck.

'Where's it gone? That gold thing you always wore.'

'I gave it to the doctor,' she said briefly. 'Drink up!'

He surprised her then by taking the mug from her hand, lifting it unsteadily to his mouth and draining it. Then he lay back, plainly exhausted from this small effort. For a moment she could see the pain in his eyes, then they cleared a little and he sighed. It was true, then, that the more he drank the less painful it would become.

She smiled hopefully at him.

'Aren't you kind to me! The doctor says the herb tea will irrigate your system and we can't move you until you're better. This isn't a very safe spot to camp. One of the men was telling me that whilst Leo and I were off fetching the doctor another train managed to cross the desert and their beasts went mad when they smelt the river water and ran amok through our tents. That was why they put you into the waggon.' She picked up the pot in which she had brewed the herb tea. 'Just one more mugful, then I'll leave you in peace.'

He sighed, but held out a hand.

'Right. Your gold thing's got to be paid for, I reckon. Whilst I drink it, go and fetch me an empty keg.'

'What on earth do you want an empty keg for?'

'I'm going to fill it,' he said briefly. 'Go get it!'

'Fill it? You aren't going to pour that good herb tea into it, are...' Light suddenly dawned and Charlotte crimsoned. 'Oh, of course, irrigation! Sorry! I'll fetch one at once.'

She got Leo to take the keg in and was

191

glad she had done so, since not only could Wolf not manage to fill it unaided, but it immediately became apparent what other function would give him pain. A positive roar came from the waggon and Charlotte could only hope that he would not behave as he had with the herb tea!

She and Leo continued to irrigate for the rest of that day and the following night and then they decided that the waggons might move on the next morning provided Wolf remained in the sick waggon.

'He won't like it, but he'll do it,' Leo said. 'I rid out for twenty-five miles ahead earlier and there ain't no good grazing that far and what's more the river winds like a crazy snake and there's a deal o' crossin' to do. We'll start early and finish late, though, and that way perhaps we'll find some grazin'.'

'Do you really think he's going to travel in the waggon?' Charlotte said sceptically. 'I bet he insists on riding Stormbird and gets thrown.'

Leo, however, shook his head.

'Nope. You sellin' that necklet for the doctor's services hit him hard. He ain't gonna be difficult for a while.'

And Charlotte, who had seen the necklet

go almost without a pang, marvelled over the mind of a man. All her concern for him, the way she had nursed him, meant nothing compared to the fact that she had given up a scrap of jewellery for his sake. That meant, to Wolf, that she had been prepared to help him, so he would do the same for her. For a while, anyway!

CHAPTER 7

The waggon train finally left the desert edge as Leo had planned it, with Wolf riding in the sick waggon and pretty well back on his old form again. He bawled Charlotte out for continuing her treatment with the herb tea when he was no longer in pain but merely a little weak, he threw a plate of thin gruel at Leo's head—it missed—and demanded pork and beans, and when none was forthcoming he stole a chunk of bread and cheese intended for someone else and made himself sick again.

'You behave like a spoilt little boy,' Charlotte scolded when she found out about the bread and cheese and got over her fear that her patient had had a relapse. 'Just forget pork and beans—and cheese too, for that matter—until you're stronger.'

'I'll never be stronger if you feed me pap,' Wolf grumbled. 'Come over here a minute.'

Charlotte innocently trotted across the waggon to his bedside and found herself grabbed, dragged to her knees and kissed with a fervour and thoroughness which had her gasping. But it seemed that it was only a demonstration of returning strength for he put her away from him and scowled at her.

'See? If I can kiss a woman giddy then I can ride my horse and eat real food.'

Charlotte scowled right back. Kiss a woman giddy, indeed!

'You can't even throw a plate straight. That gruel missed Leo by a mile! Just you stay here and eat what's given you. Don't worry, we won't starve you into submission—well, I might, but Leo won't hear of it—and you'll be riding Stormbird in twenty-four hours and eating anything you fancy.'

He lay back on his pillows, lids dropping, and smiled at her.

'I wasn't aiming at Leo or gruel would have covered his freckles. I missed on purpose. I only threw it to make a point.'

'Well, say I'm making a point by feeding you pap, then.' She went over to the bed and put a hand on his forehead. It was cool and dry. 'Please be sensible, Wolf!'

'Hmm. Do you swear I can ride tomorrow if I eat what you bring me?'

'I swear. If you can sit Stormbird, of course.'

'What's for chow, then?'

'You could have fish, Leo caught some in that trap we made, and then rice pudding. You like rice pudding, and I've got a scraping of raspberry jam somewhere.'

But apparently his burst of good humour was over. He lay down again and stared at the canvas above his head.

'Don't humour me, Charlotte, just bring me some grub.'

Hateful beast, Charlotte thought, leaving the waggon with a flounce that ill became her breeches. He and that damned nanny goat were a pair. Neither of them gave their rescuers a thought once the danger was over. She felt quite softened towards Emily for a while, having got rid of a good deal of her aggression towards the goat by

195

dragging her tail first out of the bog, but Emily was soon back to her usual tricks, nibbling Charlotte's washing, butting her if she ever turned her back, kicking over the milk bucket at every opportunity. And Wolf, when it came down to it, was just the same!

It took the full twenty-four hours that Charlotte had predicted, but the end of that time saw Wolf in the saddle once more in every sense of the words. He sat Stormbird with his usual arrogance, countermanded all the orders that Leo and Charlotte had given during his illness and then proceeded to take the reins very firmly into his own hands once more.

'It's a relief to have him bossin' again,' Leo said, when Charlotte complained. 'I ain't no nat'ral born leader, my brow's been permanently furrowed wi' worries—watch it smooth out now Wolf's back!'

'Yes, it's true to an extent,' Charlotte agreed. She was riding Tandy, glad of the hot sunshine since the constant river crossings meant that she was almost permanently damp. Up ahead of them they knew that the Rockies loomed, though at the moment they were only in the foothills, and Wolf had warned them all that once they gained height they would be struggling through snow and freezing conditions, despite the fact that it was August.

Leo bore no grudge because Wolf had vetoed his suggested camping place, either. They reached it in time to have lunch there and it was the best grass they had come across since leaving the desert's edge, yet Wolf insisted that they press on.

'How does he *know* there's better grazing ahead, and a better place to camp?' Charlotte demanded irritably as she and Leo cleared up after the meal and prepared to leave the spot. 'He doesn't have second sight, does he?'

'Guess not; guess he asked Mr Hobbs,' Leo said practically. 'Say, we'll roast him if he's wrong. That'll keep you goin' cheerfully.'

The truth of this remark was plain, but they were given no chance to 'roast' Wolf, since the valley, when they entered it just as the sunset was spreading its glow across the land, could not have been bettered. It had a placid river, grass long enough to brush the horses' bellies and tall, well-verdured trees. Everyone was pleased to be there, even Leo and Charlotte, and when Wolf announced that they would delay their departure next day so that grass could be cut and carried, since the mountains were now close enough to see distinctly, there was universal rejoicing at the thought of spending longer in such a pleasant spot.

The men began to cut grass right away and Charlotte cooked the supper alone since every man wanted to get his fodder before dusk put a stop to the cutting. Food had been running short but there was plenty of bacon and salt pork, and then one of the men came back with a dozen rabbits and she was able to make a magnificent rabbit stew, flavoured a little with salt bacon, which allowed her to conserve the rest of their meat for the mountains ahead. She considered brewing up some herb tea, then looked across to where Wolf, stripped to the waist, was cutting grass with long, even swings of his scythe, and decided against it. She did not much fancy being forced to drink the stuff herself, one of the many threats he had uttered in respect of the hated brew.

When the meal was finished Charlotte washed up, fetched water from the river and milked the goat so that the breakfast porridge could be started betimes, and then went back to her tent. Wolf was sitting cross-legged in the entrance, stitching away at a sock. Charlotte looked at the cobbled-up hole in the heel which, if he ever attempted to wear the sock, would make walking a painful business, and laughed.

'At least there's something you can't turn your hand to—give it to me, I'll mend it properly.'

Wolf handed her the sock without demur, then went further into the tent and got his clothes off, whilst she stitched in the fading light. She finished the darn off neatly, then went into the tent as well and sat down on her bedroll.

'Did you see the Sierra Nevadas?' Wolf said idly, as she began to pull her tunic over her head. 'First good view we've had.'

'Yes, I saw them. They're imposing, aren't they?'

'I guess. D'you mind heights?'

'I'm not keen, but I suppose I'll manage.' She rolled between her blankets, and then began to pull her breeches off beneath the covers. She had grown accustomed to undressing in this manner and it no longer worried her to do so with Wolf in the tent. 'But we don't go over the mountains, do we? I thought we went through them.'

'There isn't a pass. Hobbs says we'll find ourselves on ledges that 'ud dizzy a mountain goat, and it'll be no wider than the waggons in places, yet we have to pass them.'

Charlotte blinked across at him in the flickering lantern light. Why was he suddenly telling her about the hardships ahead?

'I know it's going to be tough and I don't like heights much. But I can always close my eyes and let Tandy do it all. She's a sure-footed little creature.'

'Hm. They say the valleys are littered with the corpses of mules that slip on the ledges,' the Job's comforter on the other side of the tent remarked gloomily. 'Best keep alert.'

'All right, I'll keep alert,' Charlotte said sleepily. 'Goodnight, Wolf.'

He grunted, but appeared to have run out of warnings and grim reminders of mortality and presently Charlotte dropped into a light sleep.

She was woken an hour or two later by

200

cool air entering her bedroll in some inexplicable manner. She moaned, cuddled lower, and tugged crossly at the blanket which seemed to want to slide down around her waist. It was far too cold to sit up and see why her bedding was slipping, though, and she was still too much asleep.

There was another brief moment when she was cold, and then she was warm again, warmer, if anything, than before. She was still more asleep than awake but she got the impression that someone had put an extra blanket over her and was cuddling her down once more. She mumbled 'Thank you' in her sleep, and heard a soft laugh close by her ear.

Much too close by her ear. Her heart jerked and she moved sharply, feeling an arm slide round her, a hand begin to fondle the back of her neck. The body close to her own was masculine, hard, and, unless she was very much mistaken, stark naked!

That woke her up completely. She said: 'Hey!' in a startled, rather squeaky voice and Wolf promptly pulled her right into his arms and began to kiss the soft, ticklesome side of her neck. His mouth was hot and urgent, his hands on her were firm, and to Charlotte's dismay her several reactions to this unexpected and uninvited invasion of her bed could only have made him believe it was not unwelcome. Her arms seemed to be round his neck, leaving her in a poor position to fight him off, and her heart was hammering at top speed even as she whispered 'No, no' in a most unconvincing little voice.

It evidently failed to convince Wolf. He found her mouth and if she had thought his kisses urgent before, she knew herself mistaken, for this kiss was a kiss which spoke of things to come, things she would find even more delightful if she just allowed him to take her body as he was taking her mouth. She moaned against him and he moved her a little so that he could fondle her breasts, ignoring her shirt which, in the way of nightwear, was up round her neck by now anyway.

Presently, however, he tired of her shirt. He did not pay it the courtesy of unbuttoning but simply heaved it off by sheer brute strength, making Charlotte utter a muffled protest which he completely ignored. His mouth began to move, across her throat, over the creamy skin to her breasts. She stiffened with horrified astonishment, then wriggled. It was a wriggle of protest, she told herself through the waves of pleasure which were threatening to drown all her moral rectitude, but Wolf seemed to read it as a wriggle of quite a different sort. At any rate, he made no attempt to stop the slow progression of his mouth.

After that, Charlotte scarcely knew what was happening as she clung to him, kissing, crying, drowning in a sea of sensations, all of them new, delicious, and probably very wicked. Once she cried out, but it was only a small cry, muffled by his mouth, and then he was calling her love-names, urging her to love him, love him, love him, and she was sobbing that she did love him, she did, she did, as the waves crashed on the shore and then receded, leaving her breathless, bewildered, helplessly happy.

Presently, he rolled away from her, leaned up on his elbow, and kissed her eyelids. They were little tender kisses, she thought wonderingly.

'That was...did you like it, Charlotte?'

Would he think her abandoned and dreadful if she admitted that she had liked it very much indeed? Probably he would, and probably he would be right! Vaguely, she felt that nice women should not enjoy making love; it was far too physical and exciting. But she was a truthful girl.

'Yes. I didn't know...'

Her voice trailed away as he kissed her again, this time on the side of her mouth. It made her shiver.

'I should hope you didn't know!' His voice was deep, amused. 'Want me to go back to my own bedroll, now?'

She did not answer but she put her arm round his neck and pulled until his head was resting on her breast.

That was how they fell asleep presently, and how they woke when Leo banged the breakfast pans next morning.

Later, of course, Charlotte knew she had been a fool to consent to that wild, midnight loving. Common sense had warned her how it would be if she once let Wolf possess her, and common sense was right. She knew now that leaving him when they reached California would be next to impossible, and leaving him happily would be downright impossible. She allowed herself to toy with the thought of staying with him, of getting in touch with Freddy and telling him she was here, but that she was married and would be remaining with her husband. It would be hard on him, perhaps, but he was three years her senior, he would probably marry quite soon and then where would she be?

She acknowledged frankly to herself that she was in love with Wolf, had been in love with him since well before their journey across the Humboldt desert. Sometimes, she thought he was in love with her too, but then she knew so little of men! Perhaps men did love the women they were in bed with, perhaps that was all part of the physical side of marriage. And then, when they weren't in bed, that love just died away, only to be reanimated by more lovemaking. If so, it seemed very strange, because how could one ever know when a man was really in love—the forever love that she had read about?

But it was useless to worry, because however much she might determine during the day to keep Wolf at arm's length, he only had to touch her to send such firm resolves scattering like leaves before a hurricane. She must just enjoy his loving and his company and hope that, one day, she would discover if he wanted her for always, or whether he was simply making use of her because there was no one else.

Having decided not to worry about it, she kept faith with herself and did not, which was as well since the trail now began to wind upwards, through worsening conditions, when the nights were so cold that frost formed on the men's blankets.

'Not on ours,' Wolf murmured, giving Charlotte a glance of such loving wickedness that she almost convinced herself that he loved her.

Then came an afternoon when they camped in a high and windy clearing where the spiteful cold bit deep and tempers frayed. Even Charlotte, who had been going round in a daze of happiness, felt that it was politic to get away from her companions for a while and have some peace. The men were cutting as much of the thin grass as they could because ahead of them rocks, ravines, and lonely pine forests did not augur well for grazing prospects. Wolf was annoyed with her, too, because he had found that they were almost out of flour, and the discovery that Charlotte had known but had somehow managed to forget did not make him easier to live with. So once the men were all busy she decided to go and collect firewood. It was always a cause of anxiety to the cooks on the waggon trains that they might run out of fuel and be unable to cook the men hot chow.

Her rifle was a nuisance when wood-gathering but she had been told so often by Wolf that it was tempting fate to leave it behind that she slung it round her shoulders on a length of rope, took a good, hard stare round so that she would be able to find her way back, and then went over to Wolf.

'I'm going to collect dead wood. I've got a rope so's I can tow it back, and I'll go uphill so I don't get lost. Is that all right?'

He glanced up, then nodded and gave her one of the looks that she was learning to love. It was a long, careful look, as though he were trying to imprint her picture on his mind.

'Right. Don't go too far.'

'I won't. Has Leo gone back for the flour?'

They had passed a waggon train the previous day which had been selling off surplus goods before tackling the long pull, which was another good reason why

Wolf had been annoyed to find there was no flour, but it had been a mistake to remind him. The careful look faded and he frowned, then nodded curtly.

'Yup. And I told him to get more salt pork.'

It was on the tip of her tongue to tell him that pork was the last thing they needed, that it would have been more sensible to ask for root vegetables or even for dried fruit, but she decided against it. No need to argue just because a man felt that a world which contained pork and beans was a safer place than a world which did not! She sometimes wondered if army cooks had heard of anything else, so set on those two comestibles had the men become. Not that they *liked* them, for they did not, but they took it for granted that pork and beans were to be their staple diet and were delighted when she proved otherwise.

She said nothing, therefore, but smiled, waved, and set off into the ranks of the great pines. There was little dead wood underfoot but she had not expected any yet; near a decent clearing such as the one they had camped in wood was always scarce because of the trains that had stopped there previously. She guessed that she would have a good climb before beginning to find fuel.

It was cold even in the shelter of the trees but as she climbed the exertion brought the blood pounding through her veins and made her feel quite hot. Once she unslung the rifle because she thought she heard something in the undergrowth and hoped it might be a squirrel or a rabbit which she could shoot for the pot. But nothing appeared so she trudged on upwards, going carefully over the slippery pine needles.

Presently she saw something solid, squarish. Astonished, for she knew they were a long way from civilization, she tiptoed through the trees, feeling like a character in a fairytale. She came into a clearing, and there was a log cabin, most beautifully and carefully constructed, but not, apparently, housing anyone since the door creaked half open on its hinges, showing the floor covered in a drift of dead pine needles which had blown in, probably the previous autumn.

When she walked right into the clearing she could see that there had been other cabins here too, but that they had been burnt down at some time or other and only their ashes remained. In the centre of the clearing, which she now realized must be man-made, since the logs for the cabins must have come from here, was a pit filled with ash and with what looked like the remains of bones. This must have been a permanent trappers' camp, then, where they brought their kills and wintered through the worst of the weather. Her imagination stirred at the thought of them, sitting round the great central campfire telling stories, roasting meat, cooking dampers. There had been four cabins here once. Perhaps a spark from that same campfire had blown over to the three that were no more, catching light to the dry pine logs and reducing them to ashes in no time. Then, perhaps, the remaining cabin owner had not wanted to stay here, where his friends had lost their homes, possibly even their lives. He had gone away, and that would account for the air of gloom and unhappiness which still seemed to hang, blanket-thick, over this small lost clearing.

That thought, coming so naturally on the heels of the others, quite startled Charlotte. She gave herself a mental shake.

Absurd, to say that there was an air of gloom hanging about a deserted clearing in the middle of a forest! Or, if not absurd, at least overfanciful. There was always something a little sad about a deserted homestead because you knew that people had once hoped to make their home here but had been forced to leave, to give it up, perhaps by the weather, or because the soil was poor, or even because a man and woman, far from friends and family, found that they no longer loved one another.

Charlotte walked over to the remaining cabin and swung the door wide, then peered in. It occurred to her that a family, fleeing from a place they found inhospitable even for their pioneering spirits, would be unlikely to carry their woodpile away with them. They had cut down forest giants to make their cabins, but surely the smaller branches would be used as firewood, and some might still be left, dry and usable, inside.

There was wood inside but it was already cut into short logs and though she stared at them hopefully for a full minute she could see no way in which she could rope them and drag them back to the encampment. She sighed, then turned to the door. Perhaps there were decent sized branches outside, pushed away into the undergrowth, which she might use.

She started across the cabin, which was large and airy with windows which seemed strangely high, now that she thought about it, and was halfway across the pine-plank floor when the door slammed shut. Not as it had been caught by a gust, but almost as if it had been pushed by human action. It stopped her short, her heart hammering in her throat, before she told herself not to be a fool, to remember how the wind had been blowing, and set off again over to the door.

She put her hand on the latch, and as soon as she did so she heard a sort of growling, mumbling rumble that frightened her as much as the noise of the door slamming had done. Could it be an animal of some sort—but what animal would have slammed the door on her like that? She took a deep breath, unslung her rifle, and reached for the simple wooden latch. She lifted it, and pushed against the door.

It did not give at all but resisted first her gentle pressure and then increasingly panicstricken shoves. Charlotte pushed in vain, it would not give. It must have jammed when the wind had hurled it shut—if it had been the wind.

There was silence from outside, now. She pushed against the door one more time and then went to the window, standing on tiptoe to see out. Immediately, her heart froze. There *was* something out there! A movement in the trees opposite, a flicker as something passed between two tall pines. She ducked below the sill, hoping she had not been seen. Suddenly, she no longer wanted to get out of the cabin, which had been her overriding desire some thirty seconds earlier. She shot across the room and began to heave at the huge bar which acted as a lock. It was wedged in place but still she struggled at it, heedless of splinters and bleeding fingers, desperate to bring it down into its socket. She must get it across, she must!

She did. It thundered into place just as the latch began, with infinite caution, to lift. Charlotte shrank back, her eyes fixed on the latch. It rose with awful slowness, and then the door shook as something pushed against it, first carefully, then with increasing force.

Charlotte found herself with her back against the opposite wall, shaking all over, as much with some inexplicable horror as with fear itself. She saw the latch slowly lower again and waited a moment, then, summoning up all her courage and holding her rifle at the ready, she went and stood right in front of it.

'Who's there? I've got a gun!'

Another of those deep rumbling noises, a little like a growl and a little like a grumble. Could an animal lift the latch like that, though? There were grizzly bears in the Rockies; suppose the noises were made by a grizzly? Charlotte's courage, which had been at a very low ebb indeed, began to rise a little. She stole over to the window, stood on tiptoe, and looked out.

It was standing there, staring at the door. As tall as a very tall man, covered with fur. As it turned away she saw its odd, shambling gait, saw the glint of claws. She raised the rifle, but the window was too high for a shot, and then...Charlotte dropped the gun without noticing and fell against the log wall, her flesh creeping. That creature was no bear, it was a man. She had seen his enflamed, purplish face, his rotting teeth, the hair and beard so matted and long that it was impossible to tell where one began and the other ended.

He was dressed from head to foot in skins, too, probably bearskins, which accounted for her momentary mistake. She began to tremble. It was possible for her to see out of the window, the cabin was raised from the ground. Could he get in that way? He was huge, but she did not believe that he could.

Presently, she decided she must do something. She could not remain crouching under this window for hours, or until someone came to rescue her. She stood up and looked out. He was no more than ten or twelve feet away, staring at the cabin.

'I'm sorry, stranger,' Charlotte said, 'to have to come walking into your cabin uninvited. I've friends only a short walk from here, down the hill. Would you like to come back with me, to our encampment?' There was no response; the creature merely continued to stare. 'Or...or perhaps you could go down to the camp and tell them where I am?'

His mouth stretched in a lunatic smile and she saw a gleam of calculation appear in the dull eyes. Then he hurled something at her with a roar of rage so loud that it echoed and re-echoed round the clearing, and then charged. The window was high, but even so the top of his head and his mad red eyes appeared for a horrible moment in the aperture before he fell to earth again, uttering an animal grunt.

Charlotte had left the window at a great speed; now she stopped and looked round to see what he had thrown at her. It was useless, now, to tell herself that he meant no harm. His expression as he charged and the murderous force with which he threw gave the lie to that.

The object was lying against the opposite wall. She went over to it, interest quickening. It looked like a boot belonging to a small child—and when she picked it up she saw that it was indeed a child's boot, with the sock, a bright red and blue one knitted in thick, soft wool, still inside it. And inside the sock...

She was on her knees, fighting waves of nausea, the small object flung down on the floor as if it had been red-hot. The child's sock held the browned skeleton of a child's leg from the knee down and for a moment she had held it in her hand, staring, wondering... She crouched on the floor, sick and shivering. She would not move from here, would not look out at that madman, so sick, so vile that he could hurl such a thing at her. She would stay here for ever, safe from him, until Wolf found her.

She believed, afterwards, that she was only saved from complete insanity herself by the reflection that, if Wolf came here, the madman might kill him before Wolf even realized he was not alone. She must keep watch, must warn him! So she stood on tiptoe, peering out of the window as the light began to fade, and watched as much of the clearing as she could, hoping that Wolf would come noisily, with a song on his lips.

But in fact he came so silently that he was halfway across the clearing before she saw him. He, too, must have sensed something wrong, for he was coming at a hunter's crouch, his eyes fixed on the cabin. He was concentrating on it, plainly sparing no thought for the trees at his back. He saw Charlotte and raised a hand.

'You all right, honey? What in God's name...'

Then she saw the madman, arms raised, claws as long as a bear's as he came out of the pines and prepared to spring at Wolf's unconscious back.

'Wolf! Look out! Behind you!'

Time to warn, but not time to name the danger. Wolf spun round and fired from the hip all in one smooth, terrible movement and the lunatic gave a shriek and disappeared back into the trees from which he had just emerged. Wolf gave a cursory glance behind him, then loped over to the door and rattled the latch.

'Come on, honey. Bears aren't noted for their good manners when they're wounded and I got that one. Let's get out of here!'

Charlotte opened the door and collapsed into the arms held out to receive her, shuddering with fear and relief. Wolf held her for a moment then turned up her face and kissed it.

'Come on.'

He turned Charlotte to lead her out of the clearing but she hung back, her eyes black with distress.

'We can't just go and leave him—Wolf, what did you think it was?'

'A grizzly. I saw the size of it.' She was still hanging back and he put an arm round her, half lifting her. 'Come on, let's get you back to camp and you can tell me all about it.'

She turned in his arm, part of her wanting to accept what he said, perhaps

218

even pretend she had believed it all along, another part knowing that she must tell him the truth. She clutched him, pulling him to a halt.

'It wasn't a bear, it was a man! He trapped me in that cabin, held the door shut, until I got terrified, and then I locked him out. Then he tried to get at me through the window. Please, we must search. He's quite mad, but we can't leave him lying there, wounded.'

'A man! Then Hobbs was right, there *was* a survivor from...' He looked at her, then around him. 'Did he have a weapon? A gun? A knife, maybe?'

She shook her head, as much puzzled by his quick acceptance of her story as by his questions. She knew the man had possessed no weapons or he would not have attacked Wolf with his clawed hands.

'No, I don't think he had any weapon. Wolf, what happened in those cabins?'

With the words, she had a presentiment of horror so strong that her knees refused to hold her. She swayed, then crumpled against Wolf. She leaned against him, breathing hard, her eyes fixed on his face.

'Not now, Charlotte.' He spoke gently.

'Come back to the camp and I'll bring a search party up here. We'll find the poor fellow. Now tell me exactly what happened, please?'

She began at the moment she entered the clearing right up to the time that Wolf himself had come to her rescue. She even included the object that the madman had thrown at her, though she shuddered to speak of it. When she had finished she looked hopefully up at him. Could he explain it all away, make her feel sane and whole again?

He waited until they were both back at the camp with the fire lit and the men gathered round, and then he told her, simply and without embellishment, the story of the Donner cabins. How the party of men, women and small children nearly eighty strong, had planned to cross to California but through bad management and bad decisions had arrived in the Sierras as winter was closing its iron grip on the land. How they had built the cabins, become snowed in, and starved and died there. And how they had been reduced to eating the flesh of their own dead comrades in their desperation to survive.

'So you see, my love, why the poor

devil's gone mad,' he said gently at the end of his recital. 'I'll take some men back now, with lanterns, and we'll try to find him. I'll leave Leo with you.'

'Oh, Wolf!' She clung to him. 'Must you go? Surely they can manage without you?'

But he put her from him, though gently.

'I have to go. I know where the blood trail starts. Don't fear that he'll lie out there, wounded and alone. He's gone through enough.'

It was two in the morning before the search party arrived back, and Wolf was quiet to the point of brusqueness. No, they had not found the man but they would search again by daylight. They were sure to find him then.

Charlotte had a bad night, broken by nightmares from which Wolf had to wake her. He caressed her, held her tightly, murmured sweet endearments, but by common consent they did not make love. It would have been wrong, Charlotte thought confusedly, to have been happy and together in their little tent when, somewhere out in that wild and inhospitable forest, a man was so unhappy and alone.

They searched for five hours the next day but at last they returned and Wolf gave the order to hit the trail. Charlotte had not taken part in the hunt but she mounted Tandy and prepared to ride ahead, then took her place by Wolf, mounted on a sidling, side-stepping Stormbird who was clearly longing for a gallop.

'Was there no sign of him?'

'No.' He leaned down and ran long fingers along the line of her jaw. 'Don't grieve, honey. I guess he wasn't too badly hit and got away and now he's hid up somewhere. Probably terrified, poor devil. He'll go back to his cabin once we're gone.'

But he did not believe it. The blood trail had been far too heavy. He just knew that they would never find him now, that they could waste no more time and must move on. He would leave a note in the time-honoured fashion for the next waggon train, explaining that there was a wounded lunatic at large and that the Cuban party, who had shot him by accident, had not managed to find him. That was about the best he could do. His own guess was that the poor creature's misery was over at last, that in some thicket deep in the pine forest the man's body was hidden and that one day, far, far hence, someone would find a whitened skeleton hung with skins deep in the trees and would wonder a little, maybe make up a story or two to account for it. And then forget. As they must.

They travelled on for two more days, climbing ever higher, the cold becoming more intense, the trail harder. Food was running low and Charlotte was so thin that her breeches had to have a tuck taken in the waist. Wolf's face became grimmer as they lost condition, but strangely enough he became more patient with them all, less dictatorial. They were together in a way which only comes with adversity, when all the forces of nature seem to be ranged against you.

And then she spoiled it.

The trail had been particularly harsh that day, with everything going just that little bit wrong. They had been forced to cross a river which was too deep for comfort, and a waggon had tipped on to its side. It had been righted, but bedding, a barrel of molasses and one of rice had been soaked and would probably never be quite the same again. Their first mule had died from a fall, and it had given everyone a nasty turn to see an animal they had grown to believe could not fall lying, broken, in a ravine. Lastly, when they did camp there had been no fuel whatsoever and they had not brought any with them. The cook's nightmare had come true, and hot chow would not be available, nor the means to dry out the bedding.

It was no one's fault, they were all agreed on it, but probably all of them felt a little guilty, as if, had they but known, they could have found some wood in this bleak, craggy place and brought it down to burn.

Early bed seemed the only answer and Charlotte and Wolf, both worn out and both, if the truth were known, more than a little touchy, settled down in their bedroll, now always made up together, and began to talk, desultorily, as Charlotte mended a sock and Wolf a fish-trap.

'When we get to 'Frisco,' Wolf said, dreamily plaiting rushes, 'I'll mebbe get you a gold necklet, like that one you gave the doc.'

'That 'ud be nice,' Charlotte said placidly. 'Only I think Freddy will probably replace it when...' She stopped short because there was a quality in Wolf's look which she did not understand. 'Wolf? What's wrong?'

He was looking across at her, his face cold.

'Freddy buys you nothing, d'you understand? And you won't be seeing him, either. You're nothing to him now and he's nothing to you. You're mine, remember, and what I have I damned well keep! So get any ideas you've got of seeing Freddy right out of your head. See?'

'Not see Freddy?' She stared at him, outraged. 'I *must*, I love him dearly, he's my...'

He broke across her voice, looking down at her as if he hated her.

'You think you'll get the marriage annulled, don't you? I heard you once, talking about it to Leo, saying you'd get it annulled. Well, I'll be damned if I'll let a spoilt little madam treat me like a stud stallion just because her lover's in California and she isn't!' He stood up and jerked her to her feet, prodding at her stomach with a long finger. 'You might be carrying my child by now, and even if you're not worth the trouble my son is! You'll not get away from me and go with some other feller if I have to tie you hand and foot!' She tried to speak again but he overrode her, his face pale with contempt. 'D'you think I've been fooled for one minute by your taking ways and your willing body? Not me! I can find a dozen women like you, with a good deal more class, but I bought you, fair and square, and I won't see you go to anyone else until I'm good and ready, which ain't yet!'

When he started Charlotte had almost cowered, so unexpected had the attack been but now her temper caught fire from his and she jerked herself out of his grip and shouted up into his face.

'You're wrong, you're so wrong. I'll go when I want to go, not when you're tired of me! I'll just walk out, see if you can stop me! And I'll do it, cowboy, the very first moment that we set foot on California soil. Just you watch me!'

He grabbed for her and she darted across the laced-up entrance to the tent, then hesitated. She was only wearing a shirt and it was bitterly cold outside. She turned, to see him standing watching her sardonically, so she stalked over to her bedroll and climbed into it, then addressed him over the top of her blankets.

'Now I know how you feel about me, you'd better leave me alone, that's all! Don't you try to touch me or you'll get a knife in your back!'

He came towards her, eyes gleaming, mouth changing to a shape that frightened her because of the anger and hunger in it.

'I'll take what's mine. I'll...'

A voice overrode his furious tones, a mild voice from outside the tent. It was Mr Hobbs.

''Tain't mannerly to speak to a lady like that! No sirree, specially when a coupla dozen men's listenin' in!'

Wolf stood over her for a minute, then dragged his bedding to the opposite side of the tent and got between the blankets. Charlotte lay down, shaking all over, so miserably unhappy that she longed for the release of a good cry. But she could not let him see her weeping, not when he had made it plain that he despised her so! She would have told him that Freddy was her brother, but it was useless, because he did not love her, he had said he could find a dozen women like her, had said she had used him when he must have known that

227

the truth was the exact opposite. He had used her and she had let him because she thought he loved her! The thought of his treachery brought a red mist before her eyes. He wanted to keep her until he was tired of her, and then he would throw her out—but not until she had borne him a son. She ground her teeth at the thought. She would not only leave him, she'd get the marriage annulled at once just in case she was pregnant. If she had a child, she wanted to keep it as far from its hateful bully of a father as possible. She could just imagine the way he'd treat a little new baby, sitting it on a horse whilst its mouth was still wet from it's mother's milk, roaring at it to keep its feet in the stirrups and its hands low!

A little cheered by the absurdity of this mental picture Charlotte managed to drop off and to sleep for a while, but she woke later with the feeling that he was still awake and lay in the darkness, looking hopefully across at him. If only he would come over, apologize, love her again! The whole stupid quarrel had been born out of nothing and should have died as quickly and easily.

But of course it was not as simple as that. Things had been said which she thought she could never forget, never forgive. He had turned their beautiful lovemaking into something cheap and tawdry, something that she should be ashamed of.

She slept at last, but fitfully, whilst the soreness in her heart continued to plague her.

CHAPTER 8

Even then, the quarrel might have been made up and they might have become friends again, for Charlotte was fully alive to the absurdity of it and thought, in her heart, that if she told Wolf that Freddy was her brother they might manage to understand one another again. But that was before the second incident.

Throughout the next day, Wolf said not one word to her. He spoke *at* her from time to time, always in a bullying and aggressive tone which made the men eye her with secret sympathy, but apart from that he kept as far away from her as possible.

Charlotte put a brave face on it, but that

evening, when she had finished the meal and had cleaned and put away all the pots and pans, she went and sat by herself in the sick waggon and wished she was back in England, or with Freddy—anywhere but here.

It was here that Leo found her, sitting dolefully on a box of salted bacon and crying. He climbed into the waggon, took one look at her pale, woebegone face, and put a comforting arm round her shoulders.

'Hey, li'l sweetheart, that's no way to behave,' he began. 'Come on, you didn't believe all those things Wolf said, did you? He was jest so goddurned angry...'

'Did you hear what he said?' Charlotte thought of all the cruel, untrue things, and felt so ashamed and bitter that her tears flowed faster than ever. 'It isn't t-true, Leo. I d-don't even know what a stud s-stallion *is,* but I haven't used Wolf, t-truly I haven't, whatever he may pretend.'

'Sure you don't, sure you don't,' Leo said, lifting her off the box of salted bacon and sitting down himself so that he could hold her more comfortably. 'Come on, tell Leo and then dry them tears.'

'He h-hates me,' Charlotte said, reduced to hiccups. 'H-he h-hates me and I h-hate h-him.'

'He don't hate you,' Leo said stoutly. 'But I'm bound to say he acts as if he did. Jest you tek no notice of what he said. We all knowed it were untruths.'

'*All* the men heard?' Charlotte uttered a wail of grief. 'Oh, Leo, I can't bear it!'

Leo was cuddling, cossetting and crooning when Wolf climbed into the waggon, took one long look and roared at them.

'Let go of her! Git away from him!' Since this only had the result of making Charlotte cling more tightly, Wolf grabbed her by the shoulder and dragged her across the waggon's floor. 'You're my *wife,* damn your eyes, what in hell d'you think you're playing at?'

Charlotte maintained a dignified silence, partly because she was still crying too hard to talk, but Leo stood up and came forward, looking suddenly much older than his twenty or so years.

'Don't grab her like that, Wolf, she ain't done nothin',' he said quietly. 'She's purty upset; don't make bad worse.'

'If she's upset she's got cause to be,' Wolf said bleakly. 'I'm going to bed.'

With that he turned and left them, though by the look of withering hatred which he shot at them turned Charlotte's stomach to ice.

'I'm sorry I got you into trouble, Leo,' she muttered, as they both climbed down from the waggon. 'I'll find a way to cope with it.'

'Why not tell him Freddy's your kin?' Leo suggested. 'Why not say you ain't dead set on endin' the marriage? It wouldn't do no harm to try, Charlotte.'

Charlotte, however, shook her head.

'It's no use, Leo. We've gone too far for that. We're better apart, don't you agree? All we do is quarrel.'

'I dunno. Mebbe,' Leo sighed. 'All I know is, Charlotte, iffen I'd had the luck to git you, I wou'nt have give up so easy!'

'You're a darling, Leo,' Charlotte said softly. 'We'll work something out. Good-night!'

But when she went to the tent, Wolf was waiting up for her, still cold-eyed, condemnatory.

'Leave that boy alone,' he said in a voice so low that no one else could possibly have heard it. 'D'you hear what I say? He's a decent boy and you're a married

232

woman—leave him alone!'

And with that he rolled over and went to sleep, leaving Charlotte to weep silently into her bedroll. He was leaving her nothing, not even the comfort of a friendly shoulder to cry on. At that moment, thinking of the weeks to come, she truly hated him.

The journey continued, with the trail getting progressively harder, as they had been warned it would. They crossed river beds which had known no rivers for years, with rocks that clanged and crashed as they crossed them, tipping and tilting so that waggon wheels split and the wooden waggon tongues broke off. They crossed other rivers, in full spate, rivers too deep and too narrow for the waggons to cross without coming to grief so that the men had to manhandle them across with ropes and many curses. Once, they had to lower the waggons over a precipice, and Charlotte's heart was in her mouth as she saw the men straining to bring their precious vehicles down gently, so that the whole manoeuvre was not made useless by loss.

Food was scarce and all the little extras which had enabled Charlotte to cook more interesting food either ran out or were lost in river crossings. Fodder for the animals was so scarce that they were reduced to picking bushels of leaves and feeding them to the gaunt, weary mules—and the mules ate them, too, eagerly. But they didn't thrive on them as they would have thrived on grass.

The men grew gaunt as the mules. Leo's appealing chubbiness disappeared and Wolf's cheekbones began to look as though they would force their way through the stretched skin. Charlotte knew that she was thin, too, but she hardly cared. The sharp pain of rejection had given way to a sort of perpetual dull ache and she was learning to live with it, as she was learning to live with the cold truce that her relationship with Wolf had become.

Once, coming through an incredibly difficult pass which had taken the form of a deep canyon where every shout echoed and re-echoed a thousand times, they emerged at the end of it to find a roaring, rushing river, and miners crouched on the banks, searching for gold. And finding it, as Charlotte saw when they went over to talk to the men.

After they had left the miners behind, it

occurred to Charlotte to ask Wolf if they were now in California, since the men were obviously getting gold out of the torrent.

'No,' he said briefly, not meeting her eyes. 'See Emily gets more leaves tonight. Her milk's thinning.'

And then, when they were almost at the end of their tether, they found the valley.

Wolf saw it first and beckoned everyone over. They had left the beaten trail just here, but had only deviated from it by about a mile, and they had done that because a waggon had got wedged between the rocks in a narrow ravine through which they must pass. It was not their waggon and they guessed it had not been there long, but even so they could not budge it and a way round had to be found. Now, because of that unfortunate waggon, they were standing on a steep bluff and looking down into a small, cup-shaped valley, green and lush, with a river running through it. The mules lifted their heads, sniffed, and then began to bray whilst Emily and Sally ba-aaed with happy anticipation at the thought of having a feed of real, living grass.

Charlotte turned impulsively to Leo.

'Oh, isn't it lovely, but is it real? It could be a mirage.'

Leo laughed but Wolf said curtly, 'It's real enough. Let's get these waggons organized.'

For thirty minutes, the men behaved like cats around a canary cage, prowling round and round trying to find a way in which would not wreck the waggons, and in the end they found it. At Wolf's command they unhitched the mules from between the shafts and reversed the waggons, and then the men themselves took the mules' places and began to let the waggons down the steep side of the bluff, sweating and straining against the vehicles' natural inclination to career down the slope and end up as matchwood at the bottom.

'That was kinda cute,' Leo remarked, sweat pouring down his face as his team reached the bottom. 'But, Jeez, I b'lieve it's worth the trouble.'

Charlotte, who had led the mules down the hill, her heart in her mouth all the way in case the waggons got too much for the men and simply tumbled head over heels to the bottom, nodded, her eyes wide. Having crossed the Sierras, this was like toiling through hell and arriving in heaven. Sheltered, soft, the grass grew high and there was fruit everywhere. Bitter cherry trees dropped beside the river, Charlotte recognized a great drift of raspberry canes, and there was a positive thicket of gooseberries, whilst wild roses scented the air.

'Look at that fruit!' The exclamation came from more than one mouth but Charlotte felt that hers must be the most fervent. She was longing for fruit, dying for it! She ran across to where the raspberry canes grew, taller than she and heavy with fruit, and began to pick, cramming the sweet, juicy berries into her mouth, hardly giving herself time to swallow one handful before another was at her lips.

Others were doing likewise, but presently Charlotte felt she had eaten enough raspberries and sought out the gooseberries. They were huge and luscious, a deep, translucent yellow. It seemed a miracle that they were still here, that no other party had descended that perilous bluff and stripped the bushes bare. But most of the parties would have gone through the ravine, of course, never dreaming of going a mile out of their way, especially now that they were nearing the gold country. Indeed, she supposed that, had they not been so desperate for fodder, they too would have passed the valley by rather than wasting a day or two, for it would be no easy task to get the waggons out of this Eden of a place!

Charlotte looked round her. All the men were now eating the fruit, even Wolf. Of course, they must have suffered as much as she from the lack of it, for only dried fruit had been available ever since they left St Joe's, months ago. Personally, she thought, picking a gooseberry so ripe that its skin had split, I would rather have this than all the gold in California!

By the time she was sated everyone else was at work putting the tents up and setting out the camp, but she did not feel guilty, for this was always the way of it. Then, when they had done their work, it would be her turn to do hers, to get the fire going properly and to prepare and cook the evening meal. She would make pancakes; the hens were still laying now and then, thank goodness, and she had some flour left and a barrel or more of lard.

She peered inside her tent—she still thought of it as her tent, although Wolf

238

shared it now, of course—and saw that her things had been put out for her. She rubbed her sticky hands together, then looked down at her front. Her shirt was stained with the fruit, her breeches too. She could go and fetch some water in a bucket and clean herself down...but wait, there was a cool river just over there and her clothes were dirty and horrid. Why should she not bathe in her clothing and do two jobs at once?

Wolf was at one of the waggons, helping to mend a split wheel. Because she had no desire for their cold truce to turn into hot and bloody war again, she always made sure she informed him of anything out of the ordinary that she intended to do. Now, she called out to him, her voice small and chilly as a mountain stream.

'I'm going to bathe in all my things, so they get clean too. All right?'

'Carry on,' he said without looking up. She turned and went down towards the river, bending to pass beneath the branches of the cherry trees, then breaking off a few fruits and eating them. Cherries were so delicious and these were very large.

She had nearly reached the end of the grove of cherries when she noticed something odd in one of the branches. It was a sort of lump, and she remembered mistletoe growing in an apple tree at home which looked rather similar. She stood on tiptoe the better to see it, but it was still half-hidden by the leaves, so she picked up a branch of dead wood from the ground and gave the thing a prod. What on earth was it? It seemed quite solid!

She knew soon enough. There was a high, vicious hum, a flicker of movement before her eyes, and a sharp, darting pain on her right cheek. She moved back quickly. Wasps! The horrible creatures were suddenly everywhere, buzzing round her head, her legs, her bare arms. More little darts of pain entered her flesh. She began to scream, to flail her arms. She knew the river was near but all she could see was trees and wasps. She was sobbing with pain and confusion, turning round and round, beating the air with her hands, then clasping herself as she felt the insects in her hair, crawling through the neck of her shirt, dropping down on to her bare forearms. And stinging, stinging everywhere they landed until she was burning with the agony of it, unable to do anything now except scream with the terrible, shrill scream of an animal in pain.

Wolf came. Heedless of stings and wasps he gathered her up in his arms and held her, still screaming, against his chest. She felt him begin to run, knew that she was a mass of wasps, that he would be stung too, would suffer this unendurable pain...and then the blessed water closed over her. Right over her, so that only her nose was above water. It eased for a moment the agony of the many hundreds of stings, but she could still feel wasps in her hair, on her brow, in the folds of her clothing!

'Hold still, honey!' The voice was urgent and the endearment so sweet that it almost took away the pain. 'I'm gonna duck you right under and then we'll get that darned shirt off.'

She held her breath as he ducked her, then tried to open her swollen eyes, but could not. She broke surface again, still sobbing with the pain, still only dimly aware of what was happening to her.

'There, love, they're nearly all gone. Now let's ease your shirt off.'

He got the shirt free without too much trouble and she could hear him swishing it about in the water to free it from insects, then he tied it round her by the arms, so that her breasts were covered. For the first time she wondered who else was nearby, standing near the river, but her eyelids would not lift, she could not see what was happening.

'Now, I'm gonna hold you right under, all but your nose, for another five minutes. Think you can stand it? The yellowjackets haven't given up hope of finding you again—what in hell did you do to make them so mad?'

There was amusement in his voice. She swallowed and spoke through lips swollen with stings.

'I only p-poked them with a s-stick. I couldn't s-see what they were!'

He laughed and gave her a little hug, or at least the arm round her waist tightened. It hurt, pressing the stings deeper into her flesh, but she did not care. Wolf had saved her, he was holding her, he had called her honey, love. Did he, perhaps, not hate her too much? Was it possible that he even liked her a little?

'Wolf, do you...'

'Uh-huh, here they come again! Duck, my beautiful!'

She ducked right under and he held her so for a few moments and then they broke

242

surface, gasping. They did this several times until Wolf decided that it was safe to leave the water, and then he simply picked Charlotte up bodily in his arms and carried her back to the camp.

When he reached the camp he stopped and instructed Leo to bring him a quart of vinegar and the last of the onions. Then he carried her into their tent and laid her on her bedroll. When Leo came in with the vinegar and onions he gasped at the sight of her lying there.

'Jeez, will you look at her poor li'l face! D'you want some laudanum, honey?'

Charlotte, who was beginning to feel again the agony of the stings, said faintly: 'No, not laudanum. That's for when someone shoots themselves or falls under a waggon wheel. I expect the vinegar will help.'

Leo went away, and presently, whilst Wolf was still moving round, pressing a cloth soaked in vinegar on her burning flesh, someone else entered the small tent. It was Mr Hobbs; she could smell the virulent tobacco he smoked. He, too, gasped at the sight of her stings.

'I ain't never met a gal more liable to fall right into trouble up to her neck,' he said heavily. 'I ain't sure you was wise, Wolf, to tek her to wife, but I'm bound to say I ain't met a gal with more courage, neither.'

'I'm not complaining,' Wolf said shortly. 'Why have you come in, Hobbs?'

'There's an old Indian remedy for stings—give me an hour or so and I'll mek it up for the li'l wench.'

Presently, when Mr Hobbs had gone in search of the ingredients for his remedy, Wolf got Charlotte to bed without any fuss or false modesty. There was no point in trying to hide her body from him when she thought about it. He had loved her so beautifully and so thoroughly when they were first married that there could not be much he did not know about her! Besides, she was still blinded by her swollen lids, and she felt, illogically, that because she could not see him he could not see her. So she let him bathe her in vinegar and lay thin slices of onion on the worst places and presently, when Mr Hobbs had made up his remedy which was very sticky and thick, she submitted to being spread like a slice of bread with the concoction.

'I must smell like a very odd sort of salad,' she said at one point, and was rewarded by his chuckle.

'You look like one too, honey. Won't you have a little laudanum? It would ease you.'

He must have known she was in great pain, with her face on fire and that most sensitive part of her body, her breasts, so swollen and full of wasp's venom that they felt the size of the Sierra Nevada. But she could not take the laudanum, not when someone else might need it. She shook her head slowly from side to side, feeling the tears that she could not prevent slipping down the planes of her cheeks. No, she would manage without it. Somehow.

There were several times during that long night when she nearly cried out for laudanum, though. But Wolf was so good, so patient with her! He bathed her in vinegar and in the Indian remedy, he lifted her up so that she could sip a cup of goat's milk, though the pain of the metal against her lips was severe. And in the end, though she could not know it, he watched over her whilst she slept at last.

It was two days before she could open her eyes and three before she could be moved, and never once did Wolf reproach her for holding them up, keeping them from the goldfields.

In a way, their enforced stay in Yellowjacket Valley was a good thing, because the stock ate their fill and put on flesh, gaining in strength with every hour that passed. The men, too, began to look less like living whipcord and more like men. Charlotte, lying quietly in the shade of the waggon, saw Wolf begin to lose the strain round his eyes, the harshness about his mouth. She was realizing just what a weight of responsibility he carried on those broad shoulders. Twenty-four men and a girl, a score of mules, even the cattle and the goats. They all looked to him to find them food, drink, and a safe way through country he had never travelled before. No wonder he had been quick to anger, harsh and exacting! When things went wrong he might shout and get angry, but in nine cases out of ten it was himself he blamed first. Even for the wasps—he had told her it would be all right to bathe; he should have realized that such an abundance of fruit would bring yellowjackets in its train. That he could scarcely have guessed his foolish young wife would find a nest and poke it with a stick he shrugged aside as irrelevant.

Now that they were resting in this perfect place and he was relaxed, he was thoughtful and considerate, even humorous, all the things she had told herself he could never be. As if deliberately, he was so sweet to her that she fell helplessly head-over-heels in love with him all over again, dreading the moment, now, when they would have to part.

Because kind though he was, he made no attempt to make love to her or to share her bed. And the first time Charlotte looked in the mirror she was sure she knew why. The wasp stings had taken all the glow from her skin and left it dried and flaky and her eyelids, though she could peer through them, were still red and puffy. She went to the waggon entrance and hailed one of the men working nearby.

'Tillett, would you be very kind and fetch me a lump of lard from the chuck waggon?'

The man obliged and Charlotte rubbed the stuff ruthlessly into her skin, from head to toe, though it was a painful business. It did work, though. By next morning her skin was beginning to regain its smooth, velvety texture and the colour was fading from patchy pinky-orange to its usual clear, creamy tone.

The following day they left the valley. They took a quantity of fruit with them which Leo had done his best to preserve, using Charlotte's largest pan and a good deal of sugar, and what was more important they took lively, healthy animals, capable of pulling the waggons the remainder of the way to Sacramento.

It was quite good in a way to be on the trail once more, to come across more and more miners, more and more gold claims, to know that they were on their way. But this still was not California, Wolf said, California didn't start until they reached Sacramento. No one contradicted him and, in any case, Charlotte knew they would continue their journey until they reached that town.

On the third day after they had left the Valley, Charlotte walked up the gentle incline of a nearby bluff to see whether the plains beyond the Sierras were yet in view. They were getting very close, she knew that from Mr Hobbs. It was sunset and the western sky was streaked with rose and gold, every little cloud reflecting the glory of the sun's departure. Awed, she stood for a moment watching the sky, and then turned her attention to the land, and gasped.

This must be California at last! Gentle, rolling grasslands, rivers, forests spread before her—easy country at last, good country where the stock would be able to graze their fill and the cooks would find some variety once more from pork and beans! She was leaning against a boulder, gazing with all her heart, when she felt someone's presence beside her. She did not need to look to know it was Wolf, but she looked all the same, at the high-bridged nose, the white stetson tipped on to the back of his head, the firm mouth. He saw her glance and looked down at her, unsmiling, very serious.

'I want to talk, Charlotte.'

'Yes. I suppose...' But she did not want him to talk, not if he was going to tell her that this was California and she must leave him!

'Freddy's your brother, isn't he?'

It was the last thing she expected to hear him say and it took her breath away. She stood there, gaping.

'And d'you know why I chased after that

squaw, back at Fort Laramie? Because her man was a trapper and the squaw told me he had a number of pelts which could be sewn into a cloak for you. She offered to do the job for me, so's I could give you the cloak and not a job of work! See?'

'I see. Why didn't you tell me earlier, though?'

He grinned.

'Why didn't you tell me Freddy was your brother?'

'At first I thought you knew, and then, later, there didn't seem much point. Y-you didn't seem to l-like me much, you see.' Her voice wobbled, hard though she tried to make it matter of fact. He had been leaning on the rock beside her, looking down over California, but at that he put a casual arm round her shoulders.

'Couple of obstinate mules, that's us. I could've told you that there was only one woman interested me out of the whole durned breed, and that was a chit of a redhead, who drove me mad arguing, fighting, questioning every word I said.' His arm tightened round her shoulders, pulling her close. 'Same woman who said she hated me but sold her necklace to get me a doctor, waded through a stinking bog to keep me from drowning myself, went on loving me even when I'd called her every vile thing in the book.' He took her chin and turned her head so that he could look into her face. He was serious now, unsmiling, and she could see the desperate question in his eyes. 'That's right?'

Pride had tumbled with his first words and only the love was left. She flung herself into his arms, sobbing with relief that they had bridged the gap that had somehow come between them, that there need be no more explanations, apologies or excuses. Now, truth would be quite sufficient.

'That's right! Oh, Wolf, you don't know how much I love you, nor how I've longed to be together again!'

He held her for a moment longer, then turned her face up and kissed her. It was a long kiss, but when they broke apart they were both smiling, and they turned with one accord to return to the camp. The sun had set long since and now the first stars were twinkling in a dark-blue summer sky.

'Guess I do, though. It's how I've been feeling ever since I knew how you felt—in Yellowjacket Valley.'

They crossed the encampment, deserted now, for all the men had gone to their beds so that they could leave at dawn. They walked very close, not wanting to be parted for a minute now that it seemed their differences were over. Inside the tent, Charlotte asked the question which she should have asked right at the start of the conversation, except that it hardly seemed to matter now.

'How did you find out that Freddy was my brother, Wolf?'

'Leo told me, when you'd got stung so badly. Said if I lost you, it would be nobody's fault but my own.'

'Oh. Was that the only reason you were so sweet to me—because you knew I didn't have a sweetheart waiting?'

He laughed at the pique in her tone and reached out and caught hold of her as she was struggling to unbutton her shirt.

'Here, I'll do that. I'm more accustomed to undoing buttons than you are! No, of course it wasn't the reason. Leo didn't tell me about Freddy until you were all but cured. I'd made up my mind I'd fight for you, fight dirty if needs be, but I'd get you to want me, want to stay with me.'

Charlotte smiled up at him as her shirt was cast aside.

'You knew I wanted you! You must have known it! A woman doesn't behave the way I did with a man unless she loves him...oh, terribly much!' She paused for a moment. 'Wolf! What are you doing?'

He chuckled, his mouth against the soft skin of her throat.

'What do you think? After what you just said...'

'You shouldn't pay attention to what I say,' Charlotte murmured, as he slid her between the blankets and followed after. 'Oh, Wolf, but I love you!'

'Likewise.' Wolf said briefly, beginning to kiss her.

'Wolf, wait, have you ever wished...'

A voice from outside the tent overrode her words, a deep, irate voice. Mr Hobbs.

'I wished fer a bit of peace and quiet, so's I could git some sleep afore dawnin'!'

There was a stricken silence from Charlotte, but Wolf called right back, shamelessly.

'Don't worry, feller, she's going to be too busy to talk for a bit!'

'Oh, Wolf, you're awful,' Charlotte whispered into the ear so near her mouth. 'You're awful, you're...oh, Wolf!'

The publishers hope that this book has given you enjoyable reading. Large Print Books are especially designed to be as easy to see and hold as possible. If you wish a complete list of our books, please ask at your local library or write directly to: Dales Large Print Books, Long Preston, North Yorkshire, BD23 4ND, England.

This Large Print Book for the Partially sighted, who cannot read normal print, is published under the auspices of

THE ULVERSCROFT FOUNDATION